THE ROYAL AGENTS OF MI6

DRIVE ME WILDER

BOOK TWO

USA TODAY BESTSELLING AUTHOR

HEATHER SLADE

ISBN: 979-8-88649-173-9

MORE FROM AUTHOR HEATHER SLADE

BUTLER RANCH
Kade's Worth
Brodie's Promise
Maddox's Truce
Naughton's Secret
Mercer's Vow
Kade's Return
Butler Ranch Christmas

WICKED WINEMAKERS
FIRST LABEL
Brix's Bid
Ridge's Release
Press' Passion
Zin's Sins
Tryst's Temptation

WICKED WINEMAKERS
SECOND LABEL
Beau's Beloved
Coming Soon:
Cru's Crush
Bones' Bliss
Snapper's Seduction
Kick's Kiss

ROARING FORK RANCH
Coming Soon:
Roaring Fork Wrangler
Roaring Fork Roughstock
Roaring Fork Rockstar
Roaring Fork Rooker
Roaring Fork Bridger

THE ROYAL AGENTS
OF MI6
Make Me Shiver
Drive Me Wilder
Feel My Pinch
Chase My Shadow
Find My Angel

K19 SECURITY
SOLUTIONS TEAM ONE
Razor's Edge
Gunner's Redemption
Mistletoe's Magic
Mantis' Desire
Dutch's Salvation

K19 SECURITY
SOLUTIONS TEAM TWO
Striker's Choice
Monk's Fire
Halo's Oath
Tackle's Honor
Onyx's Awakening

K19 SHADOW OPERATIONS
TEAM ONE
Code Name: Ranger
Code Name: Diesel
Code Name: Wasp
Code Name: Cowboy
Code Name: Mayhem

K19 ALLIED INTELLIGENCE
TEAM ONE
Code Name: Ares
Code Name: Cayman
Code Name: Poseidon
Code Name: Zeppelin
Code Name: Magnet

K19 ALLIED INTELLIGENCE
TEAM TWO
Coming Soon:
Code Name: Puck
Code Name: Michelangelo
Code Name: Typhon
Code Name: Hornet
Code Name: Reaper

PROTECTORS
UNDERCOVER
Undercover Agent
Undercover Emissary
Coming Soon:
Undercover Savior
Undercover Infidel
Undercover Assassin

THE INVINCIBLES
TEAM ONE
Decked
Edged
Grinded
Riled
Smoked

THE INVINCIBLES
TEAM TWO
Bucked
Irished
Sainted
Hammered
Ripped

THE UNSTOPPABLES
TEAM ONE
Furied
Merried

COWBOYS OF
CRESTED BUTTE
A Cowboy Falls
A Cowboy's Dance
A Cowboy's Kiss
A Cowboy Stays
A Cowboy Wins

Table of Contents

Part 2

Part 1

1

Wilder

"Cor blimey," I muttered when my secretary announced my four-thirty appointment had arrived.

I'd picked up the phrase up from Wellie, the head groundskeeper at my family's estate in Bedfordshire, and I'd make no apology to anyone for using the cockney expression. Alcott "Wellie" Fulton was one of the finest men I knew, and anyone who judged him differently could be damned.

"Sir?"

"Right. Sorry. Um…I'll just be another minute. Tell whomever it is to wait in the vestibule."

"I don't think so," said the woman who waltzed in and sat on the edge of my desk.

"What in the bloody hell?" I muttered under my breath.

"Wren Harlow," she said with an accent that sounded straight out of Texas, holding out her hand as though I was expected to shake it.

Instead, I leaned back in my chair and studied her.

"Well, ain't you as pretty as a Georgia peach?" I said in my best Southern drawl.

"Wrong part of the States, Mr. Whittaker, but you said I was pretty, so I won't criticize your accent too much."

"Remind me why you're here, Miss Harlow?"

I caught the eye of my secretary standing in the doorway, looking panic-stricken. "What's wrong, Mrs. Udele? You look as though you've swallowed a cockroach."

"Nothing, sir," she answered, clearing her throat and leaving my office.

"Tsk, tsk, tsk. Now you've gone and upset poor Mrs. Udele. Shame on you, Mr. Whittaker."

"As you can see by the pile of files on my credenza, I am a very busy man, Miss Harlow. So if you'd please cut to the chase, I'd appreciate it ever so much."

"I'll do so over dinner."

I sat back in my chair in the same way I had when she first walked in. "I'm previously engaged."

"Change your plans."

"Why would I do that?"

"You don't have any idea who I am or why I'm here, do you?"

I thought about looking at my desk to see if Mrs. Udele had left me a note as to why I was meeting with Miss Harlow, but the pretty Texan would likely call me out on it, so I didn't.

"As I suspected. Well, Mr. Whittaker, I am here on behalf of the United States Department of Homeland Security."

That's right. Now I remembered. She was here to talk to me about Matthew Caird, currently being held at Her Majesty's Prison Belmarsh on several murder and terrorism charges.

While the powers that be at Secret Intelligence Service headquarters agreed that Caird was more a deranged sociopath suffering from borderline personality disorder who had it out for my family specifically, the US DHS refused to relent. The bomb he'd planted in California at the home of two former CIA operatives and current contractors for the agency, meant America wanted their pound of the man's flesh.

Miss Harlow's task was to extradite Caird to the States for crimes he'd committed on their soil. It was my job to convince her otherwise and to keep the wanker imprisoned here in the UK.

"I don't know what you consider the appropriate time for dinner in your part of the world, but in the UK, we're barely out of teatime," I said.

"I can wait."

I opened the calendar on my laptop. I had nothing scheduled for the rest of the day, although I had planned to meet up with a few mates for drinks later.

"Whatever your intention may be, Miss Harlow, I can assure you that a cocktail and a decent meal will hardly sway SIS in their intransigence, nor me. Caird not only killed several of our best agents, his actions specifically targeted my family. The mere planting of a bomb at a California beach house pales greatly in comparison."

"As I anticipated, you haven't been briefed about his other crimes."

I sighed. As far as I was concerned, the woman's reason for being in my office was inconsequential. SIS would never give in, no matter what Matthew had done, didn't do, or planned in America.

However, spending an evening looking across a table at the gorgeous woman whose luscious behind was currently planted firmly on the corner of my desk might not be the worst way to kill a handful of hours.

I scribbled an address on the back of my calling card and handed it to her. "Give this to the doorman when you arrive. I'll be waiting in the bar and will instruct him to escort you inside."

Miss Harlow raised an eyebrow, but I caught a quick glimpse of a grin. She should be smiling quite broadly, given where I was taking her this evening. The establishment at Five Hertford Street was typically a place solely for the likes of George and Amal Clooney, Sir Paul McCartney, or a member of the British nobility—which I was.

2

Wren

I, Finley "Wren" Harlow, had been chosen very specifically for the assignment I was currently undertaking. According to my superior at DHS, there was no one on the team as efficient or fastidious—just like my code name indicated.

However, the government hadn't given me the nickname that became used universally in my line of duty. It was my father who'd first referred to me by the name of the active little bird whose symbolic Celtic meanings include abundant activity, vibrancy, and alertness.

"A wren is never seen resting on her laurels," he'd told me when I graduated first in my class at the University of Virginia. "See to it you aren't either."

I hadn't been, either before that day or after. One was only as good as the result of their last mission, which meant I had no intention of lowering my reputation with a failure on this one or any other.

Sutton "Wilder" Whittaker had been on my radar since I began working for the United States

Government. His older brother, Thornton "Shiver" Whittaker, former MI6 and now retired as a duke, was far more well known. It was Wilder, though, who had always intrigued me.

I'd heard through the intelligence grapevine that SIS was trying their hardest to get him to switch over to their international unit, Section 6, but so far, he hadn't moved. I wondered if Wilder had turned the job down primarily because of the man I was there to extradite. Tonight I intended to find out.

Whittaker stood, perhaps waiting for me to do the same, but I wanted to see what he'd do if I didn't. He didn't disappoint.

The swoon-worthy, handsome agent leaned all six feet three inches of his powerful body on the hand he placed on his desk almost close enough to touch my bottom. He moved so I could see his eyes which looked almost black from a distance, were really brown with flakes of gold and green. His wavy dark-brown hair had strands of blond and maybe even some gray mixed in. But mostly, his scent—a mix of sandalwood, citrus, and something else that smelled almost of aristocracy—filled my nostrils with an undeniable want.

Without needing to reach, I could slide my hand inside the folds of his jacket and run it over what I knew were the rock-hard pectoral muscles in his chest, then to his powerful shoulders, and up to cup his cheek and run my finger over the smirk on his lips.

"I'll see you at eight, Miss Harlow," he breathed, moving closer to me still. "In the meantime, think long and hard about how you want this to play out."

"Meaning?"

"Just because they call me Wild doesn't mean I don't know how to be subdued, controlled, even civilized. Although, I'd far prefer it if you chose adventurous, entertaining—even titillating."

"It's just dinner, Mr. Whittaker."

"It stopped being 'just dinner' the minute you walked into my office. You know it as well as I do."

3

Wilder

Without as much as a backwards glance, Miss Harlow left my office, leaving only the faint scent of perfume in her wake.

I smiled. The Texan bird had a hell of a battle ahead of her. Even if the case against Caird weren't personal, even if the entirety of the SIS stopped fighting his release, the UK had been lamenting the joint extradition agreement with the US since it went into implementation in 2007. Most citizens who were even aware of the treaty called it horrendously one-sided because it allowed the States to extradite UK citizens and others for offenses committed against US law—even when the alleged offense may have been committed in the UK.

Additionally, the level of proof required to extradite from the UK to the US was minimal and certainly not reciprocated.

Miss Harlow may have a treaty in hand and what she believed to be a compelling argument; however, the days of the UK submitting to US demands merely because they shouted louder were long over.

"Mrs. Udele," I said through the intercom.

"Yes, sir."

"Please see if Sir Ranald is available. The matter is urgent."

While the man most in the intelligence community knew as Rivet had been ready to retire over a year ago, he'd had no luck securing his replacement, and until he did, he was stuck.

To further complicate matters specific to Miss Harlow's mission, the man she was here to secure, Matthew Caird, was Sir Ranald "Rivet" Caird's adopted son.

It got worse. Matthew's biological father was none other than Duke Andrew Charles Thornton Whittaker, aka my father.

Last January, when our half brother had tried to kill Shiver, Darrow, and me—shortly after the duke passed away—the duchess had to confess her role in instigating the union between Sir Ranald and Matthew's mother, a woman named Anna. Why Rivet had gone along with it remained a mystery.

"Sir," said Mrs. Udele, clearing her throat as though coming to my doorway and speaking to me wouldn't be enough to get my attention.

"Yes," I responded without looking up.

"Sir Caird."

I stood and shook the hand of the man who entered my office, moved a pile of files from a chair, and sat down. I sat too and studied him. The last year had taken a toll on the Chief of the Secret Intelligence Service.

"How are you, Riv?" I asked anyway.

"Bloody knackered."

"Understood."

"Have you made any headway with your caseload?" he asked, eyeing my pile of papers.

"Not really, sir."

"Quit with the 'sir' crap, Wilder. Your mother asked me to remind you that she's expecting you for dinner tonight."

"Bugger," I muttered, pulling up my calendar. "I put it on the wrong bloody day."

"Unless you've been summoned by the queen, I don't recommend you shirk the duchess' invitation to dinner. What are your plans?"

"Agent Wren Harlow has descended on behalf of the US Department of Homeland Security. I'm to have dinner with her this evening."

Rivet put his chin in his hand and brushed his lower lip with his finger. "Well, then. You can hardly invite Miss Harlow to join you at the Kensington flat."

"Beg me off, Riv, I implore you."

"Can always say the DG summoned rather than Her Majesty."

"I heard that." In my doorway stood Archer Alexander, Director General of MI5—the United Kingdom's domestic security and counterintelligence agency, and my current boss.

"No getting me in a fix with the duchess, Riv."

"What are you doing tonight, Z? I'm sure if I drag you along, Victoria will hardly notice her missing son."

Z closed the office door and pointed at me. "From what I've heard, I should upset his plans instead."

"How's Wild's replacement coming?" Rivet asked.

"That's why I'm here, actually."

Both Rivet and I raised our heads.

"I'd like you to have a chat with Agent Marietta."

"George?" I asked, raising an eyebrow.

Z smiled. "She's more than qualified."

We'd initially called Leighton Marietta "Georgia," but it was quickly simplified to George. Z was right about her qualifications, and my hesitancy to think she could take my place spoke volumes about a misogynistic attitude I hadn't realized I possessed.

I hung my head. "As Wellie would say, I've right gone off my trolley."

Both Rivet and Z laughed, and while I had intended it to be a joke, there was a part of me that knew it wasn't the slightest bit funny.

"I'd be happy to meet with Agent Marietta. Shall I reach out to her?"

Z and Rivet both raised a brow.

"He was calling me 'sir' a bit ago," Rivet told my boss.

"I'd suggest a holiday, but there's no time."

Rivet was pushing hard for me to move over to MI6, and once I did, I knew the man would push even harder for me to take over as chief.

The job had first been offered to former MI6 agent Merrigan "Fatale" Shaw, who was now retired and living in the States with her husband, Kade Butler, a former Marine, CIA agent, and current owner of a private intelligence firm.

Next in line after Fatale had been my brother, former Marquess and now Duke Thornton "Shiver" Whittaker.

After our half brother had tried to kill him, Shiver announced his own retirement, much to the chagrin of

Sir Ranald. Although he'd been forced to admit the very public title and dukedom would greatly hinder Shiv's ability to keep a low profile as an agent or as chief.

"Sutton?" said Z.

"Sorry. Pardon?"

"I was suggesting you invite Agent Marietta to join you and Miss Harlow for dinner this evening."

I hadn't done a very good job of reining in my reaction when Z initially mentioned George, but this time I was prepared. I didn't have an answer, but at least I didn't look dim-witted.

"You could always send George in your place and make the duchess happy by not missing dinner."

Unsure whether either or both of the men in my office were serious, I decided to remove the matter from their hands and talk it over with George directly.

"Excuse me, gentlemen," I said, standing, straightening my tie, and putting on the sport coat I'd removed shortly after the lovely Miss Harlow left.

The long walk down the hallway to George's office offered me a few minutes to consider Z's suggestion about this evening's dinner.

I could ask her to join Agent Harlow and me; however, it would more than undermine my plan to convince the woman that extraditing Matthew Caird was never going to happen.

Once that was settled, I intended to maneuver the dinner in a definitively personal direction.

Before Agent Harlow's arrival, I would've questioned any suggestion that she was the type of woman who usually appealed to me. She was shorter than most I'd dated, and redheads had never held much appeal. However, there was something about the streaks of blond woven in with the softest ginger that made me want to brush the wisps of hair from her face when her bangs fell forward.

Again, while she wasn't terribly tall, when the slit of her deep-green wrap dress slid open just slightly as she planted her round and squeezable-looking tush on my desk, her legs appeared to go on forever.

If I were to describe her looks in a general way, I'd most likely say she was cute. She had a wide smile, prominent and high cheekbones, and green eyes that sparkled when she thought, even momentarily, that she had the upper hand.

It wasn't her looks that drew me to her like a powerful magnet. There was something about her aura that registered directly and immediately with the male parts of my anatomy.

No, I wouldn't be inviting George to join us tonight, I'd decided by the time I reached the door to her office.

"Come in, Wilder," George answered when I rapped on her door.

"You were forewarned." I sat down in the single chair in front of her desk.

"You could say," she responded, not looking away from her computer. "I was instructed to change whatever plans I had this evening."

"Not necessary."

"That is precisely what I told Z you'd say."

"Am I so predictable, George?"

She turned her head and met my gaze but didn't speak.

There'd been a time when I tried to woo the woman sitting in front of me much in the same way I intended to woo Miss Harlow this evening. But before we'd gotten through our first drink, she'd shut me down.

"I have no intention of jeopardizing my career over a shag, Wilder," she'd said to me that night in a way that let me know there would be no room for negotiation.

I'd often considered her the one that got away, albeit before we'd even gotten started.

It was wise on her part, given I'd been with the service longer and was also well connected through my family. It didn't stop me from wondering what it would've been like to strip away the tough exterior she presented to the world and get to know George's softer side.

"Stop it," she snapped, looking back at her computer.

"What?"

"You're imagining me sans clothes, and don't deny it."

I smiled at the faint grin on her lips. "I was just thinking that you'll forever be the one that got away, George."

"The sole woman in all of the United Kingdom to refuse to let Sutton Whittaker into her knickers."

I rested my chin on my hand. "If you ever change your mind…"

She chuckled and shook her head. "Was that all you stopped by to chat about?"

"I heard you'll soon be moving offices."

"If MI5 can ever get you to vacate."

"Z isn't quite as eager for that to happen as you are."

"He's more anxious for you to wrap up your cases, unless you intend to pass them down to me."

"I could do." However, the one that would keep me tied to MI5 couldn't be passed on to anyone, and it might be years before its final outcome was determined. "Seriously, George, I do believe Z is ready for me to brief you on the majority."

"Any but the Matthew Caird case."

"All but."

"Tomorrow, then, Wild?"

"Right. Good night, George."

Neither Z nor Rivet was anywhere to be found when I returned to my office.

"You may take your leave, Mrs. Udele," I said, absentmindedly rapping my knuckles on her desk as I passed by.

"I've reserved your table, sir."

I stopped just outside my door. Had I asked her to? Had I even told her my plans for this evening? Sometimes I wondered if the matronly woman who had been my twice predecessors' secretary had bugged the office, or perhaps she was even a double agent, quietly passing the Crown's secrets on to the highest bidder for years gone by.

"Thank you."

I watched her put on her coat, hat, and gloves through my open door. She waved, but didn't say good night or even look my way to see if I'd waved back.

I picked up my mobile rather than my office phone and called Whittaker Abbey, hoping to reach my brother.

"Wilder," answered Shiver. "How's the world of secrets, lies, and espionage today?"

"Nowhere near as exciting as you make it sound."

He laughed. "I remember all too well."

"I was visited by an agent representing US Homeland Security today," I said, knowing it would ruin my brother's lighthearted mood, but not having any choice.

"They're still determined to extradite Matthew."

"Afraid so, Shiv."

"He won't live a month if that happens."

I sighed. "The lower court is pushing to allow it."

"Has the case been moved on to appeal yet?"

"Soon, I hope."

"Push, Wilder."

Shiver's kindheartedness to the man we'd only learned existed a little over a year ago, often surprised me. As my brother frequently reminded me, Matthew was mentally ill, severely so.

"You know as well as I do that he didn't act alone, Wild. It's up to you to not only prove it, but to also figure out who actually masterminded his plans."

There were many things I admired about Shiver, but his concern over a man who tried to kill him, kidnapped the woman who was now his wife, their child, and our sister, baffled me as much as it filled me with regret. If only I could be half as magnanimous.

"American prisons are woefully inadequate to handle Matthew's ailments. Their first order of business will be to get him to give them information that he is mentally incapable of."

Without Shiver needing to repeat it, I well knew what was expected of me. If my older brother were the one investigating the case, it would most likely be solved by now.

"Rivet is pushing Z to let me go."

Shiver sighed. "It would be nice if he put the needs of the service before his own."

"Right."

"Sorry, Wild. It isn't that I don't believe you'll make an outstanding MI6 agent, and one day even chief, but this push for you to jump ship in the middle of a case that could take months to solve, is beyond self-serving."

"I thought perhaps I'd have better resources on the MI6 side."

For the second time, my brother sighed as though he were deflating. "You may be right."

"I've arranged for Agent Harlow to meet me at Five Hertford."

"Interesting," Shiver said in a voice more animated than it had been since the beginning of our conversation. "You know, there's always the possibility that the two of you are after the same thing. If that's the case, all you have to do is convince her to remain in the UK long enough that the appeal court can stop Matthew's extradition."

It was a fairly obvious suggestion, although not something that had occurred to me. Convincing her to stay on my side of the pond in order to work together on the investigation would mean my initial plan to convince the agent to let go of the idea of extradition, followed by a romp in her knickers, as George would say, would have to be curtailed. Shame.

4

Wren

I took a long look in the mirror. The outfit I'd chosen for the evening was conservative enough to be considered prudish, and that was very much by design. The words Sutton "Wilder" Whittaker had uttered moments before I left his office continued echoing in my head.

This stopped being just dinner the minute you walked into my office. You know it as well as I do.

If I closed my eyes, I could still feel his close proximity when he spoke. Chill bumps covered my well-hidden skin just thinking about the effect his voice, his breath, his body had on me.

"You know the type," Officer Sanborn from DHS had said when we'd discussed the mission. "But you, Harlow, can be counted among the women I know to have the power to resist him. You'd never let someone like Wilder Whittaker get between you and another successfully completed assignment. At the same time, I predict he'll have a hell of a time resisting you."

If the person who'd offered her opinion weren't also a woman, she would have a huge sexual harassment issue on her hands. As it was, she'd pushed the envelope of what I considered appropriate.

There was no doubt that Wilder Whittaker was suave, gentlemanly, handsome, and sexy as hell, but there were two kinds of women who I knew could resist him. The first was the most obvious—women who batted for the other team. The second, my type, was more difficult to spot.

I'd grown up in Texas, spending my days on the back of a horse, counting cattle, mending fences, and always eager to outdo my older brother in any task our father assigned. I'd never been what one would consider a Texan Southern belle. Beauty pageants hadn't been on my radar like they had for my mother, and while I knew plenty of barrel racers who had won several Miss Rodeo titles, I'd never competed.

The men who appealed to me had calloused hands, rough and rugged from a hard day's work. They were charming but in a way that made it clear that if they wanted you, they intended to have you.

Not all who came at me with that intention had been successful. In fact, there were few who could meet my list of expectations. The man who could win my heart needed to be ultra-confident, intelligent enough to carry on a meaningful conversation, and have a body with shoulders as wide as all of my home state, and an ass as rigid as a rock.

If I had any sense that I could walk all over them, they were finished before the first date. And if they couldn't outride, out-rope, out-rancher me, they never got a second.

There was no way the soft-handed Agent Whittaker could come close to measuring up, no matter how good he smelled or how sexy his English accent was. That was why I'd invited him to dinner. I knew that in less time than it took to cook a steak medium-rare, I'd find enough about him to put him in the no-way-in-hell column of men I might've once believed I was attracted to.

I'd almost walked past the unmarked door, but the sole stark marking of the number five on a plain maroon background caught my eye. Finding the door locked, I pressed the equally hard-to-find buzzer.

The doorman, as Wilder had said he would, greeted me by name and escorted me inside.

What I saw as I walked through the entry was the last thing I could've possibly imagined.

The boho-chic interior was quintessentially English with clashing patterns and prints on the carpets and walls, perhaps reminiscent of what one might find in an eccentric upper-class country home.

Eclectic art lined the walls of the various living and sitting rooms the doorman led me past, which were lit by cabaret-style table lamps and warm fires. I nearly laughed out loud when one gentleman walked by, wearing a smoking jacket and velvet slippers while puffing a Cuban cigar.

I followed my escort down a staircase to a room that could be described as more Parisian than English. Its bohemian decor was capped off by a life-size head and neck of a taxidermied giraffe. Across the dimly lit room with a *Moulin Rouge* vibe, I saw Wilder at the same moment he saw me.

"Welcome to LouLou's," he said, taking my hand and tucking it inside his arm after thanking the gentleman who had brought me to him. "I thought we'd start with a drink down here before we go up for dinner."

I took a seat on a zebra-print bar stool. "This is an interesting place," I said, looking around the room. "I can only imagine what sorts of debauchery must take place here in the wee hours."

Wilder's laugh was hearty, and his mercurial expression no doubt charmed the pants off most of the women who came before me as his date at Five Hertford.

"You're dressed quite English this evening," he said, looking me up and down.

There was little I could find about the private club online with the exception of the dress code for both ladies and gentlemen. Even then, I was uncertain whether my choice of a simple dark-red sweater over tweed wool pants, and boots that were also dark red, would be considered too casual. Evidently not, considering some of the fashion choices I'd glimpsed as I walked through the strange yet intriguing place.

"I took the liberty," said Wilder as the bartender set a glass of bourbon, neat, in front of me.

I swirled the amber liquid, lifted it to my nose, and inhaled.

"It's lovely," I said before taking a sip of what I recognized by scent alone as one of my favorites. I'd lay money that Wilder had had the bartender pour Booker's, one of the only bourbons to be bottled straight from the barrel, not cut or filtered. It was pretty powerful stuff, hard to find, but delivered a raw smokiness I loved.

As I had with the man in the smoking jacket, I almost laughed when the bartender set a martini in front of Wilder.

"How James Bond of you."

"I always saw him as more of a beer-drinking bloke rather than the type who would quell a rather mundane yet grueling day at the office with shaken vodka."

"Not that he was ever in an office."

"Precisely." Wilder studied the drink in his hand. "I envy him that," he murmured.

"From what I've heard, the position you're leaving MI5 for is even more of a desk job."

Wilder bestowed a second mercurial smile on me that quickly turned almost sorrowful. "As my brother so kindly pointed out to me earlier, I have it in me to make…what was the word he used…an *outstanding* MI6 agent and perhaps chief one day."

He looked away then, as though he was embarrassed by the admission.

"I have an older brother. We don't speak often," I blurted, surprised at my own confession.

"No?"

I shook my head and took a sip of the almost-taste-bud-singeing spicy liquid that gifted enough hints of vanilla, cinnamon, and coffee on the finish it was tempting never to swallow.

Wilder nodded but didn't speak.

I took another sip. "When I chose to further my career in Washington over riding the range and repairing fences with him on a daily basis, my brother deemed me not only selfish, but unappreciative as well."

Wilder stood, surprising me.

"What do you say we leave both of our siblings here in LouLou's and go upstairs to dinner?"

I felt the heat rise on my cheeks, wondering what had compelled me to be so forthcoming about my brother.

"Perhaps we should do this another time," I said, downing the remaining bourbon in the glass.

Wilder rested his hand on the bar and leaned in so close that I could feel the warmth of his breath on my skin.

"Never apologize for sharing something about yourself with me, Miss Harlow. I am honored that you trust me enough to do so."

"I don't ever…"

Wilder's eyes stayed focused on mine. "I don't either."

I waited, wondering, with his lips so close, if he'd try to kiss me, but he didn't. Instead, he leaned back and offered his arm as he had when I'd been escorted in.

He led me up the same winding staircase and into one of the rooms with a lit fireplace that I'd noticed earlier. Once inside, he pulled the pocket door closed behind us.

"Mighty cozy," I drawled.

Wilder motioned to the table and held my chair. The formal place setting in front of me was as eclectic as everything else I'd laid eyes on since walking into the Five Hertford. There was no doubt it was the finest mismatched silver I'd ever seen.

"Dinner will be served shortly," Wilder said, joining me at the table after making a brief call on the old-fashioned-looking phone sitting on a small side table next to the two chairs that faced the fireplace.

"May I?" He motioned to an open bottle of wine.

"Please." I watched as he poured, twisting the bottle effortlessly so as not to spill a drop as he lifted it away from my glass.

"Are all of the dining rooms this private?"

"Not at all. In fact, most of the other rooms are quite a bit larger."

He placed his napkin on his lap, leaned forward, and rested his elbows on the edge of the table.

"Please say whatever is on your mind," I said, trying to shake off my discomfort over my earlier frankness.

"I have a proposition for you."

In an act that would've been pure drama, I considered tossing my napkin on the table and walking out, but something told me that my attempt at humor might fall flat.

"I didn't phrase that very well. I didn't mean it the way you're probably thinking."

"You have the floor, Agent Whittaker. Speak your piece."

Wilder sat back in his chair. "I know that I suggested we leave our siblings behind while we enjoyed dinner, but I must admit, mine brought something to my attention earlier that I find myself anxious to give him credit for."

"And what was that?"

"He said, in essence, we both want the same thing."

He waited as though he was giving me time to protest.

"Very well," he murmured when I didn't say anything. "You want to extradite Caird to the US in order to question him about whom he was working with. The UK seeks the same information."

"And your brother's suggestion?"

"We work together."

"I assume he's suggesting that it be done in the UK."

"You are aware that Matthew is mentally ill."

"Our government would conduct their own tests to determine the validity of his illness."

"He wouldn't survive it."

"The tests?"

"The trip to the US."

Before I could ask what he meant, there was a rap at the door. Wilder waited for me to nod before he stood and slid it open.

Something that smelled absolutely divine was wheeled in on a cart and dramatically placed in front of me.

"Lobster bisque," the server announced as he removed the silver dome.

"I can assure you there is none better anywhere in the world," Wilder said as the server placed the same in front of him.

"Is there anything else I can bring at this time, sir?" the man asked.

"Nothing for me, thank you," I answered when both Wilder and the waiter looked at me.

"Shall I close the door on my way out, sir?" he asked.

"Please," Wilder answered. "Where were we?"

"Caird's extradition and our unwillingness to take no for an answer."

Wilder smiled. "There's no point in continuing that conversation. SIS will never agree to it."

"My assignment is strictly to extradite a man who is wanted for crimes committed in the United States. The treaty is quite clear—"

Wilder held up his hand. "I am aware of the extradition treaty."

"You are also aware that your own courts have determined that you must release him to my custody."

Wilder sighed. "What they determined is that there is cause for extradition. Not that he should be released."

"Same difference."

He smiled. "Are you enjoying the bisque?"

"Not half as much as the conversation."

That made him laugh out loud. "I'm disappointed that you don't appear as eager to collaborate as I am."

"You're only interested in collaboration because you know that soon the suspect will be out of your jurisdiction."

There was another rap on the door, and before Wilder could summon the person in, the door opened and someone other than the previous server came in.

"I'm terribly sorry to disturb," the man said. "But there is an urgent call for you, sir."

"Excuse me." Wilder stood, not appearing surprised by the intrusion.

When the door closed behind him, I pulled out my cell phone only to find that I had no signal. It wasn't surprising, given the exclusivity of the club; however, it left me annoyed at my inability to at least check my email.

There was something different about Wilder when he returned. I could only describe it as "lighter." Whatever the call was concerning, was obviously good news, and I said so.

Wilder smiled, again a little differently than I'd seen him do up to this point, but it left his face almost as quickly as it had come.

"Whether the news is good depends on the point of view. I'm afraid you may not find it as such."

"Out with it, Whittaker," I said, folding my arms.

"The appeal court has overturned the lower court's ruling."

"I see."

"So, unless you Yanks are ready to give up the cause, it appears you and I may have the opportunity to spend more time together."

The smile was back along with the same arrogance I'd encountered earlier in the day when I'd shown up at his office.

"You are entirely too pleased with yourself." I brought another spoonful of the bisque to my lips.

"I'll admit only to how much I know I'll enjoy the pleasure of your company."

"Even if it means it will require you being subdued, controlled, and even civilized?"

"We'll see about that."

Throughout the rest of dinner and on the ride back to my hotel that Wilder insisted he give me, he acted as though my staying in London and working the case with him here was a foregone conclusion.

I wasn't so certain. It would be Homeland Security's call whether I stayed in England or went home.

5

Wilder

The pub was crowded by the time I arrived, but I could see my mates across the room. I stopped on my way over to them to grab a pint.

"I didn't expect to see you tonight," said Pinch, clapping me on the back.

"I didn't expect to be seen." I took a drink from the glass and rubbed the back of my neck, appreciating that Axel "Pinch" Fulton had approached me before the rest of the blokes.

We'd grown up together on the grounds of Whittaker Abbey, my family's estate in Bedfordshire. Pinch's father was the head groundskeeper, whom my siblings and I had called "Wellie" since before I could remember. When I was old enough to wonder why, Shiver told me it had started because we never saw the man with anything on his feet other than Wellington boots.

Wellie's wife had died shortly after Pinch was born, so without siblings of his own, Pinch spent most of his time with us.

In a lot of ways, Wellie was like a father to Shiv and me, even more so to our younger sister, Darrow. Which made the fact that, over a year ago, Shiver and I had discovered that Pinch and Darrow were secretly dating, all the harder to navigate. I wasn't certain whether they still were, and I wasn't about to ask.

It didn't matter. Not only was Pinch my best mate, he was also a colleague at MI5—a job Pinch had gotten all on his own, even though both Shiver and I would've been glad to put in references for him.

"So…what happened?"

"The appeal court overturned the lower court's ruling on the extradition of Caird. Over dinner, I proposed Agent Harlow and I work the investigation together."

Pinch nodded. "That would change the course of the evening. Is she game?"

"She doesn't think DHS will approve it."

"You know differently."

"Not yet. It was Shiv's suggestion."

"Right." Pinch laughed. "Have another?" he asked, pointing to my empty glass.

"At least another."

"Are you staying in town?"

"Tonight, but I'm thinking of going to Whittaker Abbey for the weekend. You?"

"Undecided."

"Do I want to know why?"

"Probably not. Fancy a game of darts?"

"Always. What's the wager?"

"Pub tabs."

"Flipping hell," I mumbled. That meant Pinch had rung up quite a large one.

The next morning, I considered skipping the office and going straight to Bedford, but before I did that, I needed to know the status of the Caird investigation. Primarily, whether I'd be going it alone as I had been, or if the delightfully charming and very beautiful Agent Harlow would be joining me.

"Come in," Z called out when I walked up to the man's secretary's desk, but she was nowhere to be seen.

"Good news on the court's decision," I said, sitting in the chair Z motioned to.

"Agreed, although the rest isn't so much."

"No?"

Z shook his head. "My contact is not confident that Officer Harlow is the best person for the job, as they say."

"Did he or she say why not?"

Z sat back in his chair and steepled his hands in front of his face. "It was suggested that a man would be better suited."

I was stunned. "He said that aloud?"

"If the call itself was discovered, *she'd* be in the hot seat, not to mention what was said in it. Although she did admit she didn't necessarily agree."

"Admittedly, I am shocked."

Z shook his head. "I don't know why, Whittaker. Your reputation is…how shall I say this? Legendary."

"Mine? What have I got to do with this?"

"They're uncertain Officer Harlow will be able to resist your charms."

"Unfair on so many levels. This person doesn't even know me. Not to mention that she has such a low opinion of one of her own, uh…officers. I thought they were agents."

"Not at DHS. As far as the other matter, she does know you, Wilder, or I should say by two degrees of separation."

"Bugger me," I said under my breath. "You aren't going to tell me who it is, are you?"

Z shook his head. "Not even under threat of death."

"This person knows me only through someone else, yet she's making a determination that could affect someone's career solely based on hearsay."

I couldn't say exactly why I was so determined to keep *Officer* Harlow in London, but I felt like a dog with a bone. "What if you put George in charge?"

"And took you off the case entirely?" Z asked with raised eyebrows.

"Officially."

"My contact would never believe it."

"She might if my move to MI6 was announced publicly."

Z's steepled forefingers brushed against his lips. "And when Harlow reports that she is working with you, what then?"

"The caveat is that my role in the investigation would be classified."

"Why would she agree to such terms?"

I couldn't say why I thought she would; it was something in my gut.

"Is my involvement her only concern?"

"I can't say for certain, but it seems the only one strong enough to insist Harlow return to the States."

I racked my brain, trying to figure out who this woman might be. I couldn't remember having even minimal involvement with anyone at DHS, although that didn't mean this person hadn't moved over from another agency.

"One more question," said Z.

"Go on."

"Why do you care if Officer Harlow is replaced?"

I couldn't answer that question any better than I knew why I intuitively believed she would agree to work with me even if she had to lie to her bosses about doing so. "I can't say," I responded finally.

Z continued to study me. "I'll green-light the announcement. As officially unofficial as it may be."

"Thank you, sir." I stood to leave the office.

"Sutton?"

I stopped at my boss' use of my given name.

"Do not muck this up."

Nodding, I walked the hallway back to my office. Z's question looped inside my head. Why did I care if Officer Harlow was replaced?

"Um, sir," said Mrs. Udele as I approached her desk. "I'm sorry, sir, but she insisted."

Peeking into my office, I was delighted to see Wren Harlow's tush planted firmly on the edge of my desk.

I stepped inside and closed the door behind me.

"As I expected, I've been called back to Washington."

Rather than walking behind my desk, I stood next to her. "Shame. When do you leave?"

"In the morning."

I attempted to contain my smile, hoping against hope that Z would be able to work his magic before then.

"You seem pleased."

"Not at all. In fact, I am profoundly disappointed."

"To be honest, I am as well. My guess is it would've been fun to see who won out in the end."

"What do you mean?"

"Come on, Wilder. It wouldn't have been a competition to see whether Caird ultimately remained in the UK or we prevailed as I anticipate we will?"

Competition be damned. All I could think about at that moment was how much I wanted to lean closer, breathe in her scent, even touch her lips with mine. But I couldn't. Whoever Z's contact was, predicted I'd do exactly that, and when I did, something told me that

Wren would be lost to me forever. Inexplicable pain settled in my chest just thinking of it.

"Your reaction is a far cry from twenty-four hours ago," I said.

Wren stood and straightened her charcoal-gray pencil skirt and reached for the jacket she'd tossed on the chair. "One day older, I suppose."

"Wait." I rested my hand on her arm.

Our eyes met: hers questioning, mine struggling.

I ran my free hand through my hair while the other remained on her arm.

"There's to be an announcement soon. I'm not exactly certain when. However, I will be moving on from my position with MI5."

"To Section 6?"

"Yes."

"Sooner than you anticipated?"

"Much."

She moved her arm away. "Congratulations, Agent Whittaker."

I was at a loss for words. Whatever my brain came up with sounded too much like a come-on. "Perhaps we could celebrate over lunch?"

Wren looked at her watch. "I don't know what time lunch is at in your part of the world, but for me it's barely past breakfast."

I grinned. "Right. How's the Black Dog at…let's say twelve noon?"

I held my breath when she hesitated. Was she really going to turn me down, walk out of my office, and then what? Be angry when she realized, tomorrow, that she'd been duped? That was if Z was successful in convincing whomever the wretched hen was who was insisting Wren leave.

"I was going to do some sightseeing, but I suppose I could squeeze in lunch."

"You know, I fancy some sightseeing myself."

"I would think you'd have seen all of London by now."

I picked up her jacket, held it for her to slip her arms into, and leaned forward. Everything about this woman assaulted my senses in the best possible way. My hands lingered on her shoulders a moment too long, and in that time, I swore I heard her breath catch.

I closed my eyes against the temptation of resting my head on hers, backed away, and motioned to the door. Since I parked underground, I hadn't bothered with an overcoat when I came in.

"Fancy a drive?" I asked.

"I was killing time anyway," she murmured. The softness of her voice surprised me. Perhaps she was sad about having to leave.

"What time is your flight?"

Wren laughed, and the sound was like the most beautiful symphony to my ears. "It isn't until tomorrow, Wilder. I've told you that twice now."

"Morning or afternoon?"

"Again, already answered, but can I ask why it matters?"

"It's a bit of a long drive." I led her off the lift and over to the passenger door of my 1967 Jaguar XKE.

She didn't respond, but she didn't hesitate getting in the car either when I opened the door for her. To me that was a win.

"There's something I need to tell you," I said a few minutes into the drive. I could see her gaze from the corner of my eye.

"Go ahead."

"The Caird investigation will be officially handed over to MI5 Agent Marietta."

"And unofficially?"

I smiled. She was quick—another thing I liked about her. "Whatever involvement I may have in it will be on a need-to-know basis only."

"Meaning you'll still be leading the investigation, but no one can know about it."

"That's right."

"Because of your move to MI6?"

I shook my head and looked out the window, taking a deep breath before continuing. "No, Miss Harlow, because of you."

6

Wren

"If you didn't want me to divulge that information, you could have refrained from telling me."

"Bollocks," he mumbled, scrubbing his face with his hand. "This may be premature, but there is a negotiation taking place that may change your travel plans."

I turned in my seat so I was looking directly at him. "Why?"

He let out a deep breath. "Because I don't want you to leave London."

"And yet you're heading north on the motorway."

He bestowed on me one of his mercurial smiles. "Better put, I don't want you to leave England."

"Why not?"

He sighed again, and the smile disappeared. "I don't know."

I looked away, unsure whether I should confess feeling the same. "Where are we going?" I asked a few minutes later.

"There's a pub in Bedford with food so out of this world, it's not to be missed."

He rolled his eyes when I snickered.

"Okay, the truth is, I want to show you the abbey."

"I was hoping that was where you were taking me."

Wilder slowed the car and pulled off the motorway.

"I may not know a lot about this part of England, but it doesn't look like we're in Bedford."

"We aren't." Wilder stopped on the side of the road and killed the engine. "There's more I need to tell you," he said, unfastening his seat belt and turning his body toward me.

"We'll be working together, Miss Harlow. That's if everything goes the way I hope it will. And that means as much as I'm dying to kiss you right at the moment, I cannot."

My cheeks flushed. I wanted to look away from Wilder, deny how much I wished he would go ahead and do it, but I couldn't tear my gaze from him—and that fact annoyed the hell out of me.

Wilder leaned his head against the back of the seat. "I hope you understand that stopping myself from touching you is literally killing me. The last thing I should be doing is taking you to my family's estate or even spending the day with you. However, I am powerless to do otherwise."

His fingertips touched my cheek, and I leaned into his hand.

"Open your eyes and look at me, Wren."

"Wilder…start the car."

He did as I asked, and got back on the motorway.

By Texas standards, Wilder's familial estate was on the smaller side, but it was beautiful nonetheless.

"Pinch's father is the head groundskeeper," Wilder said, perhaps noticing that I kept looking from left to right, taking it all in. "You should see it in spring and summer."

"I can only imagine."

While Texas was, in my opinion, one of the prettiest places I'd ever been, this was too, but in such a different way. It wasn't as though I hadn't seen formal gardens, or even the English countryside. It was almost as if I could envision Wilder exploring every nook and cranny of this place when he was a young boy.

"I'd love to know what you're thinking right now."

"I was picturing you growing up here."

The mercurial smile was back. "Do you ride, Miss Harlow?"

"You're joking."

Wilder raised a brow. "I suppose I should've asked if you ride *English*."

"I'd prefer bareback."

"Over anything?"

"Over English."

"You may be in luck. I've heard my sister, Darrow, has been riding Western as of late."

"Why?"

Wilder shook his head. "My question precisely," he muttered. "As with many things my younger sibling does these days."

"I'm not exactly dressed to ride, Wilder."

The way he looked me up and down set my skin first on fire and then ice, as chill bumps rose on its surface. There were countless reasons I could name why Sutton Whittaker wasn't my type, without even trying. That he was known as Wilder should've crossed him off my list from the get-go. And yet, my body seemed to be in complete disagreement with my mind, and it was pissing me the hell off. No one got under my skin. No one.

"You're Darrow's size."

"You're so certain, are you?"

When I turned toward him in anticipation of a witty comeback, Wilder looked more embarrassed than playful. "My apologies," he murmured.

"For what? You've said far worse to me than guessing I'm the same size as your sister."

Wilder turned his head away. "My apologies for that as well."

"Don't worry, Whittaker. I've handled men far worse than you've been."

He pulled up in front of what had to be the abbey and turned off the engine. "Have I been that bad? Truly?"

This was perfect. I hated contrite. If a man did something to apologize for, he should make it sincere, quick, and be done. Did he expect me to coddle him, tell him it was okay, say he needn't worry?

I'd turned my head away, but looked back, and when I did, Wilder's face was an inch from mine.

"Because I can tell you, little bird, I am known to be much, much worse."

The tone in which he said the words struck a chord that ran the entire length of my body, finally settling in a pool between my legs.

There was nowhere for me to go inside the small car. If I backed away, I'd only be an inch farther than I was now. My mind raced, seeking something that could abruptly change the mood.

"This is where it happened, isn't it?"

Wilder leaned back, as I'd hoped he would.

"Not the abbey per se. Caird was detained at Covington House. We'll go take a look after I show you the main house."

I waited while he got out, walked around, and opened my door, holding out his hand to me. Rather than take it, I lifted myself off the seat and stood in the small space between the Jaguar and his body. It wasn't that I didn't appreciate him being a gentleman; it was more that I didn't trust myself to touch him.

"Detained is an interesting word choice," I commented as he led me to the ornate front door.

Wilder didn't open it. "While I'm certain this is likely common knowledge, I have never told anyone that if it had been up to me, Caird would be dead."

"And yet, you don't want him extradited to the States, because you fear he wouldn't survive it."

He shook his head. "My brother—the man whose decision it was that he stayed alive in the first place—fears Matthew wouldn't survive it."

"I see."

"I'll forewarn you, Shiver and his wife, Orina, are in residence. If you'd rather not participate in a debate about extradition, we probably shouldn't go inside. We could always walk the grounds instead."

"What about your sister? Is she here?"

Wilder nodded. "Up for a walk?"

"Always." I pulled my phone out of my bag when I heard the familiar ringtone indicating it was my office calling. "Excuse me."

"Wren, I'm glad I could reach you. I'm calling in regard to the developments in the Caird investigation," said the assistant director.

"Yes, I'm scheduled to leave London tomorrow morning."

"About that. We think it's best you stay on in the event the United States is successful in re-appealing the appellate court's decision. In the meantime, you can continue your investigation."

I turned around and studied Wilder; his eyes met mine.

"You'll be working with MI5, specifically with Agent Leighton Marietta."

"Yes, ma'am." This news wasn't unexpected, given the conversation Wilder and I had had on the drive from London to Bedfordshire.

"Agent Marietta is expecting your call to arrange a meeting."

"Is there anything else I should be made aware of regarding this case?" I asked, wondering if she'd make mention of Wilder's reassignment.

"Not at this time."

I turned off my phone and put it back in my bag. I couldn't risk the possibility of anyone overhearing the conversation I was about to have with the man standing in front of me with a sheepish look on his face.

"As you may have guessed, my itinerary has changed again and I will, officially, be remaining in London."

Wilder nodded with scrunched eyes.

"I've been instructed to make contact with Agent Marietta."

"Yes."

"What exactly is your role in this investigation?"

"There is only one way my role is changing."

I folded my arms and waited for him to continue.

"No one from your government can know that I'm still leading it."

"Are you suggesting I lie?"

"What I'm suggesting is there's a good chance you'll be reassigned if they're made aware."

7

Wilder

I watched as an ethical war played out on Wren's face. It was unfair to put her in this position, although the choice was hers in the end. She could give me up, report to DHS that they were mistaken about my involvement, or lack thereof. Or she could keep quiet about it and remain on the case.

No report coming out of either MI5 or MI6 would divulge my involvement; I'd see to it.

"You mentioned we might be able to ride?" she asked.

I smiled. "Let's see if we can find Darrow and get you some proper attire."

"I'd appreciate that."

"Wren?"

"Don't," she said, holding up her hand. "I'm not ready to discuss Caird or my role in the investigation."

Rather than walking the rest of the way to Covington House only to find her not home, I rang my sister.

"I heard you're out roaming the estate with a very attractive woman." I could feel Darrow's smile through her voice.

"Wondering if she might be able to borrow something to ride in."

"Yes, of course, if you think…"

"What?"

"I was going to say something ridiculous like 'if we wear the same size,' but that is one of your gifts, isn't it?"

I laughed, not knowing exactly what she meant, but assuming enough to know it wasn't a conversation I wanted to continue with Wren in such close proximity.

"Be there shortly. Thanks, Darrow."

"You and your sister are close," Wren said when I rang off.

"You could say. However, there's a great deal about her life I'd rather remain in the dark about."

"Intriguing, and not the first time you've been mysterious in her regard."

"Let's just say I hope Pinch Fulton isn't at her place and, if he is, that he is properly clothed."

"Oh!" Wren laughed. "That is intriguing."

"Or completely ridiculous. Depending on the point of view."

We walked the rest of the way in silence. Every so often, I would brush her hand with mine and our eyes would meet. The one time I'd apologized for it, she told me not to.

When Darrow opened the door and invited Wren in, I saw I wasn't far off in my estimation that the two women were the same size. In fact, they looked to be the same height and weight almost exactly.

Once I'd made introductions, I excused myself to the loo, giving them time to retreat to my sister's wardrobe, or whatever they were going to do.

When I returned to the main room, I could hear them talking and laughing from upstairs.

I wished I'd forewarned Darrow that Wren and I were work colleagues only, but she may have seen through the lie anyway, at least on my part.

My sister came downstairs alone.

"She's lovely," said Darrow, winking.

"Stop it."

"What? You do realize that this is the first time you've brought a woman to the abbey since you were in upper school."

"Don't be ridiculous, and please lower your voice."

"It's true," she responded, leaning closer. "I see why, though. She's…nice. Not exactly who I might've expected, but better."

I looked up when I heard Wren's footfalls on the staircase. My sister was right. She was lovely, and unlike most of the women I'd dated, she was completely down-to-earth, comfortable in her own skin, and probably rarely fussed with things like hair and makeup. I found everything about her refreshing.

"Ready, then?" I asked, holding my arm out by habit, surprised when she took it.

"Enjoy," said Darrow, waving as we left. "Oh, I already called the stables."

I smiled and shook my head. "She can't help herself."

"From?"

"Meddling."

The barns were partway between Covington House and the abbey, and when we approached, I saw two horses, Domino and Pirate, in the pasture.

"This is Pirate," I said as the horse sauntered over to meet us at the fence. "He's never been known to ignore a beautiful woman."

Wren held out her hand and then obliged by scratching his forehead when he nudged her with his muzzle.

Domino raised his head when I whistled and called out his name, but the horse didn't budge. "He's a stubborn one," I said, walking over to the gate.

"Come on, boy," I heard Wren holler and watched as Dom walked straight in her direction.

"You must be joking," I muttered under my breath and glared at the horse. "Way to make me look like a wanker."

We walked to the barn and tied the horses a reasonable distance apart. Without me saying a word, Wren made her way to the tack room and chose her own curry comb, dandy brush, and hoof pick.

"I hope you don't mind." She carried the pad, saddle, and headstall, slinging it over a stall door near where she'd tied Pirate off.

"Not at all," I murmured, smiling to myself.

I watched as she brushed the horse's back and girth, keeping her touch light and her tone soft while she talked and continued to clean the rest of him.

When she ran her hand down Pirate's leg, he bent his knee and stayed perfectly still while Wren cleaned his hoof.

I wasn't half as far by the time Wren had her pad brushed and was checking the saddle. She caught me looking and smiled.

"I know a lot of people would rather skip this part, but it actually relaxes me as much as the horse."

"It shows," I said, turning back to finish getting Domino ready for our ride.

Once we were both on horseback, I motioned to an area on the other side of the barn. "My favorite trail is up there. It'll take us to the back of the abbey."

As she and Pirate followed, I could hear her talking to the horse, but not well enough to know what she was saying. When we came to a clearing, Wren eased Pirate into a trot, quickly followed by a gallop.

"Ready, boy," I said to Domino, easing him into the same.

"Thank you for bringing me here," she said when we slowed at a narrowing of the path. "In so many ways, it reminds me of home, yet it's equally as different."

"You're welcome," I answered simply when what I wanted to say instead was how much I loved seeing her here, how happy and relaxed she looked compared to when she'd ended her earlier phone call.

Riding up to the abbey, I saw Shiver walk out of the atrium that ran half the length of the main part of the house.

"You must be Miss Harlow," he said when we walked the horses over and dismounted. The two shook hands after I took Pirate's reins and led both horses over to the fence to tie them off.

"She's on holiday," I told Shiv.

My brother raised a brow. "Didn't you just arrive?"

"It's a very short holiday," said Wren, smiling over at me. "In fact, I'm afraid once we return the horses, it will be at an end."

"Pity, Losha was anxious for a double date this evening. Even talked the nanny into staying on later."

"What about Darrow? She couldn't watch him?" I asked.

"It was actually a triple date Losha arranged. Is that a thing? A triple date?" Shiver looked at Wren, who shrugged. "Darrow and Axel will be joining us."

"That's on, then?" I sniped.

"Appears so." Shiver cocked his head. "Is there an issue I'm unaware of?"

I glared at my brother. "I forgot. You're the guy that nothing ever bothers."

"Happily married, mate. You should give it a go."

Good God. Was Shiver serious?

"What do you say, Miss Harlow?" I heard Shiver say to Wren.

I cleared my throat and was about to intervene when I heard her respond that she'd love to join them.

"I can still beg us off, you know," I said once we were back on horseback, headed to the stables.

"If you'd rather not go."

"That isn't it. I'm just…" I shook my head. "You. I'm just worried about you."

"Worried?"

"That isn't it either." I hung my head not understanding why I couldn't either stop talking or think of something intelligent to say.

"Wilder. Look at me."

I looked up to find she'd brought Pirate to a standstill. "If you'd rather not do this, I can get a car back to London."

Not knowing what else to do, I dismounted, tied Domino to a tree, and walked over to her. Wren climbed off Pirate, holding his reins.

"The thing is," I began, cupping her cheek with my palm. "I can't think straight."

"Why not?" she whispered.

I leaned forward and did the exact thing I knew I shouldn't do, told myself I wouldn't do. When I kissed Wren, instead of pushing me away like I thought she might, she wrapped the arm that wasn't holding Pirate's reins around my neck and kissed me back.

Once I began, I couldn't stop. I'd spent most of the last twenty-four hours thinking about how her body would feel pressed against mine, what she would do when I thrust my tongue into her mouth. I couldn't get enough. I angled my head and went deeper, wrapping one arm around her waist while the other caressed her face.

I pulled back and rested my forehead against hers. "I won't apologize for that."

Rather than answer with words, Wren brought her mouth to mine a second time, kissing me with the same vigor as I'd kissed her. Her hand that held the horse's reins, wrapped around my waist, pulling my body into hers.

"Don't tell me this means you've decided to return to America," I said, resting my forehead against hers a second time.

"Has anyone ever told you, you talk too much?"

I smiled, wishing I could kiss her again, tell my brother we wouldn't be having dinner with them after all, take her to Dorchester House, and keep her there for days.

"I have to know," she said.

"What must you know?"

"What's behind your shit-eating grin?"

"Whether I can keep you locked away until tomorrow, or if we'll have more time than that."

Wren dropped her arms, turned around, and climbed back on Pirate. "See you at the barn, Whittaker."

Before I could respond, Wren and Pirate were gone with the wind.

8

Wren

I pushed Pirate hard, but no harder than I knew the horse wanted me to. I wondered how often Wilder's sister rode him, given the horse seemed to be accustomed to my height, weight, and riding ability. Confident rider, confident horse, my father used to say.

When I didn't hear the other horse behind me, I found myself disappointed that Wilder wasn't in hot pursuit. Or maybe that was a good thing. That kiss—okay quite a few kisses—was off the charts, hotter than all get-out.

Now what I needed was something to balance out my feelings for the man whom, as of tomorrow, I'd be working the Matthew Caird investigation with—at least on the surface. That wasn't all, though. I needed Wilder to show his true colors, so I could get him out from under my skin.

I recognized that at least half of my attraction to him was that I couldn't have him—or shouldn't. It wouldn't be long before his English-nobility-ness turned me off entirely, and then it would no longer be about being unable to have him. By then, I wouldn't want him.

As I got closer to the barn, I slowed Pirate down to cool him off. When I leaned forward and scratched his neck, he whinnied.

"Thanks for the ride, Pirate man," I said. "I'll have to remember to thank Darrow for letting me hang out with you."

"Darrow had nothing to do with it," said Wilder, coming out from inside the barn and startling me. "Pirate is my horse."

"You took a shortcut."

The mercurial smile was back. "I did."

"It would've been far more interesting had we raced."

Wilder walked closer to Pirate and scratched just above his muzzle. "That's what you expected me to do. What fun would that have been?"

I dismounted, tied Pirate off, and began removing his saddle and pad.

"I can do that," Wilder offered.

"No need. I told you before that caring for a horse before and after a ride relaxes me."

As Wilder walked back to Domino, it was impossible not to notice how hot he looked in the snug breeches I hadn't realized until now he was wearing. They emphasized his rock-hard glutes and hugged his powerful thighs. Even his riding boots were about the sexiest thing I'd ever seen, though if asked, I would've said I'd much prefer a man in Wrangler jeans and cowboy boots.

"Be careful what you wish for, Miss Harlow," he said, drawing my attention from his behind up to where he was looking at me over his shoulder.

I ran my gaze back down and then up his body. Wilder smirked and walked away, muttering something I couldn't hear.

"What was that?" I called out to him.

He shook his head, waved behind him, and proceeded to remove Domino's saddle and pad, brushing him down like I was about to do to Pirate.

"You're such a good boy," I said, walking the horse back to the stall with the steel plate bearing his name. Pirate was the perfect name for a horse that belonged to Wilder, who reminded me of Johnny Depp's swashbuckling character, Jack Sparrow. Only the man who owned the horse I rode was a hell of a lot hotter.

I stood outside the stall, stroking Pirate's forehead and getting lost in the memory of how Wilder had kissed me. I flushed and shivered simultaneously. Was I fantasizing his arm snaking around my waist, pulling me back against his hard body? No, this was far too vivid.

I opened my eyes when his lips touched the back of my neck.

"What I said was, it looks as though I'm going to have to set some rules, Miss Harlow."

"What would those be?" I murmured, loving the feel of his hands as he moved them from my waist and down my hips.

"No more visibly lusting after me unless you're certain we're alone would be one."

I wanted to say he was flattering himself, but every word he spoke was true. I had been lusting after him. I still was.

"What else?" I breathed.

One of his hands cupped my bottom while the hard tip of his tongue ran from just below my ear down my neck, until his chin rested on my shoulder. "I reckon there should be some kind of punishment when you do."

He sunk his teeth into the soft skin of my shoulder, and I groaned.

"That would work," he muttered. "Or this."

He squeezed my ass hard enough that I yelped.

"Yes," he said. "Both of those will work."

"What about you?"

"Are you referring to my punishment?"

I nodded.

"You are punishing me every second of every hour I'm with you. Keeping my hands off you, not peeling every stitch of clothing from your body and laying you down naked before me, is the absolute worst kind of torture."

"Wilder—"

"Shh," he whispered. He turned me so I faced him. He rested his hands on my shoulders and kissed my forehead. He took my hand in his, pulling me away from the stall door. "Shall we explore some more of the…property?"

Property? Did he say property? Right now, the only exploration I wanted to do was of his body. His naked body.

Wilder stopped walking and pulled me into his arms. "My sweet, beautiful Wren, make no mistake. I want you as much or more than you want me. And when the time is right, I'll have you."

His words should have annoyed me. I should be setting him straight that under no circumstances would he *have me*. Instead, every inch of my body craved his touch. Yearned for it, in fact.

"Sanborn was right," I whispered. "You are intoxicating."

Wilder dropped my hand and took a step back. "What did you say?"

"My boss at DHS. She warned me about you." I took a step back too and wrapped my arms around my waist, suddenly feeling a chill when only moments ago I felt as though I was on fire.

"Amanda Sanborn?"

"Yes," I nodded, immediately realizing what Wilder's reaction to the name meant. "The two of you…"

Wilder shook his head. "Not in the way you're thinking."

"How many ways are there? Wait. Don't answer that. I don't want to know." I shook my head like he had, feeling as though I'd been doused with a bucket of cold water. It jarred me out of my stupor just in time. A few minutes more and I might have stripped naked for him right in the tack room.

I stomped off, not knowing exactly where I was going, only that I had to get away from Wilder Whittaker as quickly as possible. The humiliation, embarrassment, and anger I felt over not being able to resist him made me sick to my stomach. I was above this. *Amanda Sanborn* of all people.

I couldn't say I hadn't been warned. More than once, in fact. I knew the danger of letting Agent Whittaker get too close, but—God—I was only human.

"Wait," he called after me. "Let me explain."

I kept walking. "Whatever that was, will never happen again," I said over my shoulder. "In fact, I'd like you to take me back to London." I could see Darrow's place in the distance. "I need to get my clothes," I said, picking up my pace.

I knew within minutes that he didn't follow me. Like when I was riding Pirate back to the barn, I vacillated between relief and disappointment.

I wasn't through the gate to his sister's house, when Darrow came out the front door.

"Is this a bad time?" I asked, remembering what Wilder had said about the possibility Pinch might be there.

"Not at all. Come in, and we'll have a cup of tea," she said, putting her arm through mine and leading me inside.

"I'd rather have a shot of bourbon if you have it."

"I have something even better," she said, pulling an unmarked bottle from a shelf in the kitchen.

"What is that?"

Darrow pulled the cork from the bottle, poured two glasses, and handed one to me. "Wellie makes it," she said, downing the shot in her glass before I'd barely taken a sniff. "He's…how do I bloody describe him?" she said, pouring herself another shot.

"Your boyfriend's father?"

Darrow laughed. "Yes, that will do for now."

By the time we'd finished our third shot, I knew that if I didn't slow down, I'd regret it. I hadn't eaten much all day other than fruit for breakfast and this much alcohol on a mostly empty stomach was never a good idea. I turned my shot glass over on the table. "I need to eat something."

"Good idea." Darrow stood and pulled cheese and fruit from the refrigerator.

"Can I help?"

Darrow pointed to a cupboard. "There's bread and jam in there. That should fill our stomachs at least until dinner."

"Oh. There's been a change of plans. We're no longer going to dinner. I need to return to London."

"Yes, I know. I've been tasked with changing your mind."

"You won't be able to." I filled a plate with bread, fruit, cheese, and jam while Darrow turned the fire on beneath a tea kettle.

"We should've started with tea," she said, joining me at the table. "Now, tell me about you and my brother."

"There's nothing to tell."

Darrow leaned back in her chair and laughed. "What a load of rubbish."

"We have to work together. Actually, we don't. I can still leave."

"Whatever are you going on about?"

"One of the reasons I was assigned to this case was the powers that be believed I was capable of handling Agent Whittaker. They were wrong. In less than twenty-four hours, he had me almost begging him…" I looked up. "I'm sorry. He's your brother."

"It's okay. I'm used to it." Darrow shook her head. "That isn't right. When I was younger, all my schoolmates would swoon over both my brothers. Over Axel too, but back to Wilder. I suppose there was a time he was a bit of a ladies' man, but he's been different since…you know…the thing with Matthew Caird."

"I'm sure that was very hard on all of you."

"It was, but not in the way you're thinking."

"He says that a lot."

"What? 'Not in the way you're thinking'?"

I nodded.

"Makes sense, given most people immediately jump to the wrong impression of him."

"My impression was right; I just let him dissuade me for a few minutes."

"Now, see? That's what I mean. You probably think he's a douche, but you're wrong."

"He had an affair with someone I work with."

"Are you certain?"

"One hundred percent."

"Based on what?"

I told her about the meeting I'd had with the woman and then about Wilder's reaction when I said her name.

"Hmm."

"Come on, Darrow. You can't doubt they at least had sex."

She shrugged. "I'll admit it would be easy to jump to that conclusion, but you did say he said it wasn't what you thought."

"Right. He'll probably say she was in love with him, and to him, it was just sex."

"Look, you have to work with him, right?"

"Maybe."

"Come to the pub with us, let him know you're no longer interested, and then set the stage for what comes next."

"Meaning that we work the case together and nothing else?"

"Exactly."

It sounded simple, but something told me it would be far from it.

9

Wilder

Instead of following Wren to Covington House, I went in the opposite direction, to the abbey.

"Hello, Losha," I said when she greeted me at the front door. Kazmir stood next to her, holding on to her leg. I leaned down. "How's my man today?" I asked, holding up my hand for Kaz's high five. The boy slapped at my palm and then spun around in search of something. A few seconds later, I heard his squeal of delight when his nanny came around the corner and surprised him.

"They've been playing hide and seek," my brother's wife explained. "Are you looking for Shiv?"

"I am, unless I'm intruding."

"Last I knew, he was in the kitchen, explaining to Mrs. Mollybock why we won't be dining at home this evening. Evidently, she knew you were here and planned a grand dinner."

"I'll go talk to her," I offered, knowing I'd have to promise to come home next weekend, or she'd be in a tizzy.

When I walked into the kitchen, Shiver was rubbing the back of his neck with his hand and Mrs. Mollybock looked as though she was getting ready to pummel him with a wooden spoon.

"There he is," she squealed much like Kaz had, dropping the spoon and scurrying over to me. "How are you, Sutton?" she asked, looking me up and down. "Too thin, I see."

"I'm fine, but I do miss your cooking ever so much." I met my brother's gaze over the cook's head. I'd always been her favorite, and when we were younger, it didn't sit well with either Shiver or Darrow, particularly when she'd make the dishes she knew I liked so often that even the duke and duchess had complained.

"The duke tells me you're dining out this evening," she said with her hands on her hips.

It always took me a minute to remember that people weren't referencing my father when they mentioned the duke; they were speaking of my brother.

However, Mrs. Mollybock had known Shiver and me since birth, so that she called him the duke, seemed odd.

"I'm here to discuss our dinner plans with my brother, in fact."

Shiver was out of the kitchen ahead of me even though he'd been farther from the doorway.

"I swear that woman was going to hit me with that bloody spoon."

I laughed. "It did look like she was about to."

"It isn't funny." Shiver tried to scowl, but I knew behind it was a grin. There was very little that bothered my brother these days. At times it was annoying, but after everything he and Orina had been through, seeing them both in love, living here at the abbey with their son, warmed my heart.

I often wondered if I'd ever find someone to love in the way Shiver loved Orina. He would've gone to the ends of the earth for her, and he had.

For several months, she and the baby had been in hiding. At the time, Shiver didn't know about Kazmir, but now, the two were expecting their second child in early summer.

"Where's Miss Harlow?" Shiv asked once we were well away from the kitchen.

"I believe she's with Darrow."

Shiver raised a brow.

"We had a…how should I say this? An awkward conversation."

"About?"

"Amanda Sanborn."

Shiver looked puzzled.

"You remember—"

"Yes, of course I do, but why were you and Miss Harlow discussing her?"

"Her name is Wren. Actually, it's Finley, but that's beside the point. Amanda is her superior."

"Amanda went to DHS?"

"It appears so."

"Bloody hell," Shiver muttered. "I told you at the time you should have had Z report her."

I shrugged. "I figured we'd go our separate ways, not thinking for even a moment that our paths would cross again."

"I'm not surprised the NSA let her go. Evidently, Homeland Security either isn't aware or doesn't care that she's…"

"Let me fill in the blanks, Shiv. The woman is bat-shit crazy."

Shiver took a seat in the room that used to be our father's study and was now his.

When I sat, Shiver got back up and walked over to the fireplace. "Does it seem cold in here?"

"It does, but then, it always did."

He lit a fire and then sat back down. "Amanda Sanborn," he muttered. "Never thought we'd hear her name again. She was a bit of a stalker if I remember correctly."

"A bit?"

"How did she come up?"

I explained the conversation, leaving out the part where Wren and I were close to tearing each other's clothes off. Instead, I cut straight to the part when she muttered the woman's name.

"Wren assumed I'd had an affair with Sanborn and stomped off, unwilling to even let me explain."

"And you think she went to Darrow's."

"I know she did."

"What's to do, then?"

I ran my hand through my hair. "I really like her, Shiv."

I expected my brother to scoff, perhaps remind me that I'd only known the woman for two days, but he did neither.

"You'll be walking a fine line, Wild, but you know that. There are times when it can't be helped."

In our line of work, it wasn't uncommon for MI6 to work with the CIA, even intelligence agencies from other countries. It also wasn't unusual for romances to blossom between agents, operatives, or in Wren's case, officers. When Shiver met Orina, she was an assassin for United Russia hired to kill him. Instead, they fell in love. It wasn't that simple, but falling in love never was.

"I'll say it again, Wild. What's to do, then?"

"I don't want her to leave."

"Do you think she will?"

"A distinct possibility."

Shiver ran his finger over his upper and lower lips as he often did when he was deep in thought. "You could always tell her the truth about what happened."

This time I scoffed. "Right."

"You have cultivated quite the reputation."

"I haven't *cultivated* it."

As Shiver well knew, it had been over a year since I'd pursued any woman in the way I once had.

Since our mother had been forced to confess that our father had been sleeping with a girl from the town of Bedford and had gotten her pregnant in the months prior to their marriage, the idea of sleeping around turned my stomach.

Matthew Caird was the byproduct of that affair, and he had lived a troubled life, not necessarily because of it, but because, as we'd learned after she died, his mother had also suffered from borderline personality disorder like Matthew did.

The idea that I might unwittingly father a child with a woman I wouldn't want to marry, made me hesitant to even date, let alone leave the pub with someone I knew I'd have sex with and never see again.

"She wants me to take her back to London."

"Now?"

I nodded.

"Perhaps Darrow can talk her into staying for dinner."

"That was my hope."

By the time I heard from Darrow, I was convinced she'd driven Wren to London herself.

"Don't be silly. We got to talking."

"Does she still want to leave tonight?"

"Hang on," my sister whispered. "Okay, I've gone outside."

I rolled my eyes at my sister's attempt at being covert. "What's happening, Dar?"

"Wren is joining us at the pub for dinner."

"Okay."

"She's going to re-establish what she says has to be a purely professional relationship between the two of you."

Rather than feeling like the thirty-five-year-old man I was, I felt like I was reliving my adolescence. "Do you think she intends to stay on the case?"

"Oh, yes."

"What makes you say it that way?"

"Anyone who spends an entire afternoon rehashing and convincing herself that she has to stay away from you, will likely not be able to."

"Thanks, Dar."

"Wren and I will meet you at the pub at eight."

I checked the time. It was half past six now, leaving me with more than an hour to kill. On my way out, I confirmed the time with Shiver before going to pay a visit to the man who had so often served as a surrogate father to me.

"It's good to see you, my boy," said Wellie, welcoming me into the small house the Fulton family had lived in on the estate for generations.

"How are you, Wellie?" I asked, returning his embrace.

"Same as I always am. What brings you here?"

It wasn't long before I finished telling him the story I'd told Shiver. In the same time, I'd had two shots of the man's homemade brandy.

"What is meant to be, will be," he said, rubbing my shoulder.

"Ah, the elder speaks his wisdom."

"You know what you have to do, Sutton. You don't need me to spell it out for you."

"Could you please anyway?"

"Do as she wants. Work the case, be professional, do not, under any circumstances, attempt to seduce her."

"We're having dinner at the pub tonight, Wellie. Join us?"

"No, no," he said, getting up from the table and walking into his sitting room. "I'm happy to stay here and eat the stew Mrs. Mollybock brought over. The same feast I'm sure she prepared in your honor."

I smiled, wondering as I often did whether Wellie and the cook were sweet on each other. Not that I'd ever ask. "Fancy a fire?" I asked instead.

When Wellie nodded, I stacked the wood the way he'd taught me, added kindling, and struck the match. It wasn't long before the fire was roaring and Wellie had nodded off.

"Don't forget your stew," I said, rubbing his shoulder.

"You're off, then?"

"Yes, in fact, I'm late."

"Don't forget what I told you."

"Right. No seduction."

10

Wren

When Darrow and I arrived at the pub, I looked through the crowd at the bar, expecting Wilder to be waiting like he had been at Five Hertford, but I didn't see him.

"Shall we get a pint while we wait?" Darrow asked. "I'm sure the others will arrive any moment."

"Let's, but nothing stronger than beer tonight."

I put my hand on my stomach, thinking it might be wiser if I skipped alcohol altogether. I'd never been accused of not being able to hold my liquor, but Wellie's moonshine packed an unexpected wallop.

"I can get it," I offered when Darrow approached the bartender.

"Don't be ridiculous. Black and tan okay?"

"Thanks. I'll get the next round."

Out of the corner of my eye, I saw Darrow look at her watch and then pull out her phone while she waited for our drinks.

Every time the pub door opened, I caught myself watching for Wilder, and it was pissing me off. I never should've let Darrow talk me into sticking around for dinner tonight. How rude would it be to call for a car back to London and leave now? I wouldn't leave my new friend here alone, but once someone else showed up, I was out of there.

Darrow came up beside me and handed me a glass. "Here's to cheating, stealing, fighting, and drinking."

I laughed. "One of my father's favorite toasts. If you cheat, cheat death. If you steal, steal a *man's* heart, in our case. If you fight, fight for a brother. If you drink, drink with me." We clinked glasses and I took a sip.

In a short amount of time, the pub got crowded enough that I could no longer see the front door.

"Oh, there's Axel," said Darrow, putting her hand on the back of a bar stool and standing on her toes to look over the mass of people. "Huh, I don't see Sutton, though. Maybe he's coming with Thornton and Orina."

Or maybe he wasn't coming at all. Now that Pinch, or Axel as Darrow called him, had arrived, this would be the perfect opportunity to say a hasty goodbye and head back to London. I couldn't remember ever waiting around for a man, and I wasn't about to start now, especially for someone like Wilder Whittaker.

"It's bloody crowded in here," I heard Shiver say, and looked over to see him taking his wife's coat before removing his. "Hello, everyone."

"Where's Sutton?" Darrow asked.

"I thought he came with you," Shiver answered, looking at Pinch.

"Why would you think that?"

"Last I knew, he was headed over to see your father."

I put my hand on Darrow's arm. "Listen, I'm not feeling all that well. I think it would be better if I got a lift back to London now."

"Oh. Right…um…do you want Axel to take you?" Darrow looked deflated, but I couldn't let that dissuade me. After all, we'd spent the entire afternoon together.

"I can call for car service."

"What's this?" asked Shiver, coming back from the coat check.

"Wren is going back to London."

"No, no," said Shiver. "We're having dinner. Come now." He took my arm and led me in the direction of the dining room. "I'm sure Wild got caught up with Wellie and is just running a bit late."

"It isn't that…"

Someone greeted Shiver, and since he was no longer listening, there was no reason for me to continue. I would've taken the opportunity to leave, but he still had his hand on my arm.

"Our table's ready," he said, giving me a little push to follow the barmaid at the same time Darrow appeared next to me, linking our arms.

Pinch pulled out a chair for me first and then for Darrow, sneaking a kiss on her cheek as he did.

While everyone else was being seated, I checked my phone. It was a quarter past eight, which meant Wilder was only fifteen minutes late, but that he was late at all rankled.

I never dreamed he'd stand me up for dinner, but maybe he was. Not that he was standing me up alone; it seemed everyone was puzzled by his absence.

An awkward silence descended on the table. Was it my imagination or was everyone sneaking uncomfortable glances at me?

I had wound up seated with my back to the door, not wanting to be rude when Pinch held my chair, but I always sat facing the door. He and Shiver, even Orina, were probably the same way. It made me just as anxious as the empty chair next to me.

When all those sitting across from me looked up at the same time, I knew Wilder was standing right behind me. I let out the breath I hadn't realized I was holding when I heard him apologize for being late.

"I got caught up with your father," he said, squeezing Pinch's shoulder, who was seated on the other side of Darrow.

Instead of walking toward me, Wilder went in the other direction, saying hello to Orina and Shiv.

"Excuse me," I murmured, setting my napkin on my chair and leaving the table in search of the ladies' room. Once I found it, I went inside and rolled my shoulders, knowing it wouldn't come close to relieving the tension spreading throughout my body.

I looked in the mirror, horrified at how pale I was. I almost never wore makeup, but tonight I wished I had; Orina and Darrow were outrageously beautiful. Rarely did I care about measuring up to any other woman, but tonight I felt…inadequate. To my chagrin, my eyes filled with tears.

I splashed my face with cold water, resolving again to sneak out without Wilder and his family noticing.

I could send his sister a text letting her know I felt worse, not better, so I left.

I turned my back to the mirror and rested against the sink, realizing too late that it was wet when I felt a chill spread across my backside.

That was the nail in the coffin of what had promised to be a nice day but ended up a miserable one. I flung the door open with my mind firmly made up. I was leaving.

"Wren, please accept my apology for being so late. I truly did get caught up with Wellie," said Wilder, who was leaning against the wall directly in front of me.

"You don't owe me an explanation."

"I feel as though I do, about more than my tardiness."

"I'd really rather not—"

"I didn't have sex with Sanborn," he blurted.

I folded my arms.

"I wouldn't lie about it," he added.

"You didn't do a very good job hiding your reaction when I mentioned her name."

"As I said earlier, it wasn't the way it may have seemed."

"Look, if anything, it served as a wake-up call. I'm here to do a job, Agent Whittaker, not to add another notch to your scratched-up bedpost."

His head snapped back just slightly as though my words had slapped him. "Wren...I..."

Had I really stunned him speechless? That hadn't taken much.

"Wilder...I..." I stammered like he had. "I need to make it clear that nothing is going to happen between us. I got swept away this afternoon, and I don't intend to let it happen again. If anything, I owe you an apology."

Wilder quickly masked the brief glimpse of hurt, and in its place was a steely expression.

"Very well," he murmured. "Shall we rejoin the group?"

"Actually, I told your sister earlier that I'm not feeling well. I'm going to skip dinner and head back to London."

"Of course. I'll let the others know."

"Good night, Wilder," I said, walking over to get my jacket from the coatroom.

"What? No. I'm taking you back to town."

"That isn't necessary. I'll hire a car."

"Not in Bedford at this time of night, you won't. It's no trouble. I brought you here, promising your safe return."

"I'd rather make my way on my own."

Wilder put his arm around my shoulders and led me back into the less-crowded hallway.

"Is this because of the thing with Amanda? I swear to you that nothing happened between us."

"It isn't that. Well, it is. Do you know why I got this assignment?" I asked, shaking my head and wondering why in the hell I was still talking.

"Why?"

I glared at him. Was he really trying not to smile?

"It wasn't the whole reason, but in part, because I don't do this, Wilder. Men like you don't affect me. I don't know what happened this afternoon, but it won't happen again." Hadn't I just said the very same words? Why was I repeating myself? Who was I trying to convince?

"Join us for dinner, and then I promise I'll give you a lift back. The truth is, I'm famished. I swear we'll make it quick."

Arms still folded, I studied him.

"Come on," he said, tugging at my arms. "Let's end your brief holiday in a controlled and civilized manner."

I fought against smiling at the words he'd used yesterday in his office. Could that really have been only yesterday?

"Okay," I murmured, "but we have to make it quick." I turned to walk back to the dining room and felt Wilder's hand on the small of my back. I should shrug it away, but I couldn't bring myself to lose the warmth that spread through my body from just his simple touch, particularly given the chill of the cold water I'd sat in.

Wilder held my chair, his body brushing against mine when I took my seat. I was beginning to understand why women fell so hard for the MI5 agent. The man was intoxicating. Instead of succumbing yet again, I squared my shoulders, determined to get through this dinner as I would any other where there were work colleagues present.

"I took the liberty," he murmured when the waitress brought me a second black and tan and one for him. "Cheers," he said, raising his glass to mine.

"Cheers," I responded before setting my glass back on the table.

"You have to take a drink," he leaned over and whispered. "Otherwise, you negate the toast."

Without thinking, I raised my glass and took a sip. I saw Wilder wink, and turned my head, catching Darrow smiling at her brother.

"Did you two enjoy your afternoon?" he asked.

"I'd say," said Pinch. "They were three sheets to the wind when I stopped by."

"Don't lie," said Darrow, laughing and leaning back against him. "We were nothing of the sort. Well, maybe just a little, but we did take a break for tea."

I could feel Wilder's gaze resting on me. It filled me with as much warmth as his hand had on our walk back to the table.

I turned my head to study the menu, taking great pains to slow my breathing and will the flush on my cheeks away.

"You're lovely when you smile," he whispered. "You're lovely when you don't, too."

"Please, Wilder, don't do this," I whispered in reply, closing my eyes.

"I wish it were that easy," he said, looking at his own menu. "The fish and chips are outstanding."

11

Wilder

I smiled as my sister coaxed another story from Wren about her family's ranch in Texas. Soon the two were laughing so hard it was impossible for the rest at the table not to laugh too.

"Tell them about the lightning," Darrow said, fanning her face.

Wren shook her head. "I'm sure everyone is getting tired of my stories."

"You have to tell them this one. You must."

Taking a swig from her third—or was it fourth?—black and tan, I'd lost count, she and Darrow began laughing again before Wren got started.

"Come on now," said Pinch. "You have us all on the edge of our chairs."

"Okay, okay." Wren took a deep breath and wiped away the tears that came with her absolutely adorable giggles and then cleared her throat. "Wait, one more sip." She paused to take a drink and then scooted her chair back an inch or two from the table.

"My brother woke me up one night, yelling something about a storm and saying that our pa was out in the barn with the cows." She made eye contact with Darrow, who was already laughing so hard she was holding her stomach.

"My dimwitted brother pulled me out of bed and out of the house in the middle of not just a storm, but it was thundering, and lightning was striking pretty damn close to our ranch. We made a run for the barn and found our pa, just like he'd said, with the cows."

Wren took a deep breath, trying to stop herself from laughing.

"You can't stop now!" shouted Pinch. "What in bloody hell was your pa doing with the cows?"

"Okay, okay," she repeated. "He'd gone out to the barn before the storm, thinking he could get a jump on our next day's work, which was…" Wren couldn't continue, she was giggling too hard, and Darrow looked as though she was going to fall off her chair.

"He was…artificially inseminating a cow when a bolt of lightning hit the back of the pens."

"Tell the rest," Darrow pleaded.

"Just as we got inside, a big ball of electricity came hurling toward Pa and the cow. He'd just finished depositing the bull's semen and got the head catch open. Quint and I watched that cow go flyin'. She got blown straight outta that chute."

"That isn't the best part," said Darrow. "The bloody cow actually got pregnant!"

The further she'd gotten in her story, the more pronounced her accent became, which I found as adorable as her giggles.

"Tell them the one—"

"No," begged Wren. "I can't. No more stories." She was holding her stomach. "My belly hurts."

My eyes met Shiver's. My brother smiled and nodded as though he knew exactly how I was feeling in that moment, and he approved.

"Can I get anyone a nightcap?" asked the barmaid.

Wren looked at me and shook her head. "I've had too much already."

I looked around the table as everyone shook their heads. "Just the tab, thanks."

"I'll get our coats," said Shiver.

"Will you get ours too?" asked Darrow, handing our brother her ticket.

"I loved your stories," I said, leaning closer to Wren. She weaved just slightly, perhaps from all the laughter, maybe it was the alcohol, or a combination of both. She looked as though she could fall straight to sleep.

"Would you still like to return to London tonight?" I asked, brushing her neck with my fingertips.

She leaned into my caress and pulled out her phone. "It's so late."

"Tell me what you want, and I'll gladly do it," I whispered.

Wren bit her bottom lip and closed her eyes, and when she did, I was transported back to earlier in the day when we were in the barn, ready to rip each other's clothes off. Before she'd mentioned her boss.

I leaned closer, and when she opened her eyes again, I was near enough that I could feel the warmth of her breath. It would be so easy to kiss her.

She brought her lips to mine and then abruptly pulled back. "God, what am I doing?" she said more to herself than to me.

"Shall we go?" I asked when Shiver returned with our coats.

"Please."

I stood and held her chair at the same time Pinch did the same for Darrow.

"I'm so disappointed you're going back to London tonight. Perhaps I can convince you to come back next weekend. I so enjoyed our afternoon."

"As did I," Wren answered, returning Darrow's hug.

"Promise you'll bring her back, Wild."

"I'll gladly do whatever Wren wants," I said as I had moments before.

I rested my hand on the small of her back, guiding her out the pub's door after we'd said good night to the rest of the group.

"I made a fool of myself tonight," she mumbled as she waited for me to open the passenger door of my car.

"You did not."

"I did. I'm sure I bored you all with my ridiculous stories."

I leaned into her, cupping her cheek and looking into her eyes. "You were brilliant. Darrow loves you, and so does Orina. It was abundantly clear. Shiver and Pinch were equally enthralled." I caressed her cheek with my thumb. "You already know that I'm your biggest fan."

She swayed a little and rested her head on my shoulder.

"Let's get you home." I moved her away from the door so I could open it, and helped her inside.

"How much did I have to drink?" she asked when I got in the other side.

"Three or four pints over the course of about the same number of hours."

"I feel as though I had twice that." She turned in her seat and studied me. "You didn't put something in my drinks, did you?"

"I'd no more do that than I would lie to you, sweet Wren."

"I wasn't serious," she murmured, closing her eyes and resting her head against the back of the seat. "I know you wouldn't."

She opened her eyes when the car came to a stop and I shut off the engine.

"Did I sleep all the way back?" she asked.

"Yes, but we didn't go as far as London."

"Where are we?"

"We're at the abbey, although not actually at the abbey itself. This is Dorchester House." I got out of the car and came around to open her door.

"Why are we here?"

"Because you need rest."

"Wilder, I can't…"

"Shh." I put my finger to her lips. "This is a big house with several bedrooms. I can either sleep in one where you are not, or I can go up to the abbey and spend the night. Whichever you'd prefer."

"You don't have to go to the abbey."

I smiled. "Let's get you inside and into bed." I put my arm around her shoulders and guided her through the gate and to the front door.

"You really are sweet," she murmured as I stepped inside, turned on the lights, and reached for her hand.

"Sweet?" I put my hand on my heart. "You wound me, woman. Please, I beg you, don't let that get out."

I came back downstairs after getting her settled and poured myself a brandy. My guess was Wren had fallen asleep the minute her head hit the pillow.

Only bothering to turn on one light, I went into the sitting room and lit a fire. I sat in the closest chair and watched as the flames bounced off the crackling wood.

My resolve when it came to Wren lasted only as long as I was away from her. If she was close enough to touch, I couldn't resist. If I moved closer still, I had to fight against grazing her skin with my lips.

The only thing stopping me from climbing the stairs and crawling in bed with her was that I'd promised I'd sleep where she wasn't.

Resting my head against the back of the chair, I took another sip of Wellie's brandy and closed my eyes, remembering how good she tasted, how soft she felt when we'd kissed out on the trail during our ride.

I'd been in a constant state of arousal throughout dinner, which was only made worse by thoughts of what might have happened at the barn if she hadn't mentioned Amanda Sanborn.

My eyes opened when I heard footfalls on the creaky stairs and turned to watch as she looked for me.

"Wilder?"

"In here, sweetheart." I didn't get up, wanting to see what she'd do if I didn't.

"I was wondering...I mean...I'd like a drink of water."

"Of course," I said, getting up.

"I can get it. Stay where you are."

I sat back down and listened to her puttering in my kitchen. I heard her turn the faucet on, then off, followed by the sound of her padding back in my direction.

Would she go back upstairs without saying anything else, or would she come in and talk with me? I prayed she'd do the latter, if only to get one more glimpse of her in the shirt I'd given her to sleep in. It was long enough that the tails touched her knees, but that didn't make it any less sexy.

"Am I disturbing you?" she asked, sitting in the other chair that faced the fireplace.

"On the contrary."

She smiled and took a sip of water.

"Although, I expected you to be fast asleep."

"I was, but then…"

"What happened, Wren?"

"I had a dream."

I closed my eyes and rested my head against the back of the chair as I had only a few minutes earlier. "Of?" I asked.

"You. Me. The barn."

I opened my eyes and looked into hers. "I had the same dream, only I wasn't asleep."

She sat back and looked into the fire. "I tell myself over and over to keep my distance from you," she murmured. "But I can't."

"It isn't any easier for me."

"What are we going to do, Wilder? How are we going to work side by side, day in, day out?"

Her voice was laced with a combination of frustration and sadness. It was the sadness that tore at me.

"Earlier I said that I'd do whatever you wanted, Wren, and I meant it. But..." The one thing I knew would make things easier for her would be to let her work directly with George. It was the only thing I couldn't do.

If it came down to choosing the investigation or Wren, it would be the hardest thing I'd ever done, but I'd have to let her go. I owed it to my family. Until I knew whom Matthew had been working with, or for, I couldn't ensure their safety.

"I'd recuse myself before I'd ever ask you to," I heard Wren say as though she could read my thoughts.

My disappointment was palpable when she stood to leave.

"Good night," I said. "Sleep well."

"I'm not ready to say good night."

I looked into her eyes. "Wren?"

Without answering, she turned and walked away, much as she had when she left my office yesterday. Had that really been only yesterday?

12

Wren

When I opened my eyes, it was daylight, although the sky outside the window looked dark and dreary. It wasn't unusual for England, especially in January.

I rolled over in the luxuriously comfortable bed and buried my head under the pillow, not so much because of its pounding ache, but more because I'd spent several hours tossing and turning while every humiliating thing I'd done yesterday looped in my head.

The culmination, the icing on the cake, the *coup de grâce,* was when I'd gone downstairs for "a glass of water," and all but invited Wilder to come to bed with me.

What in the name of all that was holy had I been thinking? I couldn't blame it on the alcohol; I'd told him soberly I wasn't ready to say good night.

I'd never forget the look on his face when he said my name. The combination of regret and pity had sent me scurrying upstairs without another word.

After my endless protests, telling him again and again that nothing could ever happen between us, I hadn't been able to stop myself from going downstairs, hoping when I went back up, he'd be with me.

We would return to London today. He'd drop me at my hotel after our horrendously awkward two-hour drive, and then probably turn right around, returning to spend the rest of the weekend with his family.

I wished I'd gotten up at sunrise and sneaked out for a walk on the grounds, given I'd likely not be invited back.

Deciding it was time to face the music, I got out of bed and padded across the hallway to the bathroom. After washing my face, I returned to the bedroom to change into the same clothes I'd worn yesterday.

I didn't hear or see any sign of Wilder when I crept downstairs. Maybe he was still asleep and I could sneak in a walk after all.

As I got closer to the kitchen, the heavenly scent of coffee wafted through the air and into my nostrils. Bless him for his kindness, I almost said out loud.

Near the French press sat cream, sugar, and a note.

*I regret that I've been called back to London
on an urgent matter. Darrow will bring you
into town whenever you're ready.*

His sister's number was scrawled on the bottom.

An urgent matter. Was that a euphemism for I'd rather avoid seeing you this morning?

I poured a cup of the still-warm coffee, added cream, and pulled out my cell.

"I thought you'd sleep much later," said Darrow when she answered.

"I'm sorry, did I wake you?"

"Good heavens, no. With all the commotion this morning, I couldn't go back to sleep after Axel and Wilder left."

"Commotion?"

"Didn't Wilder leave you a note? How did you know to ring me?"

"All it said was that he'd had to return to London on an urgent matter."

"I see." Darrow let out a deep breath. "I'll be over in a sec. Better to tell you in person."

I looked at my phone, stunned that Darrow had ended the call so abruptly.

A few minutes later, I heard a knock at the door.

"Come in," I hollered before realizing it was probably locked. I rushed over and opened it.

"Hi."

"Hi," Darrow answered, hanging her head. Gone was the friendly, fun, outgoing woman I'd met yesterday. In her place stood a woman who appeared to have aged overnight.

"Tell me what's happened," I asked, leading Darrow into the sitting room where Wilder and I had sat together the night before.

"It's Matthew Caird. He tried to hang himself last night."

"Tried?"

"The guards found him in the nick of time it seems. He's in hospital now."

"I see." My head spun with Darrow's report. Caird had attempted suicide? I mentally shook my head at the possibility.

Why hadn't Wilder woken me? Weren't we supposed to be working this investigation together? More questions flew through my brain, but Darrow wasn't in a position to answer any of them.

"My brother said to bring you to town whenever you were ready."

"I won't trouble you. I'll hire a car."

"I'm going anyway. I've been summoned to the Kensington flat. Would you like to leave now?"

"I have a couple of calls to make, and then shall I meet you at your house?"

"I can wait." Darrow went into the kitchen.

I checked the time. It was the middle of the night in the States, and a weekend at that. I'd likely have better luck waiting to contact my team once I was in London. In the meantime, perhaps I'd be able to reach someone from SIS who could give me more information about Caird's condition.

I went upstairs and dialed Wilder's number; the call went straight to voicemail. The same thing happened when I tried Agent Marietta and when I called the man most knew as Z.

I was getting angrier with every passing minute, but that wasn't the fault of the woman who was waiting downstairs to give me a lift.

I thought back on my conversation with Wilder about how it had been Shiver's decision to let Caird live the night he almost wiped out most of the Whittaker family. I wondered how Darrow had felt at the time. Had she agreed with Shiver about sparing the man's life?

"I can hire a car to take both of us. I'm sure this is very upsetting for you," I offered when I went back downstairs.

"I'm fine," Darrow said, walking out to the car. "Stiff upper lip and all that," she mumbled.

"I'm not English. You're welcome to cry on my shoulder, yell and scream, whatever you feel like doing. I can assure you, we aren't expected to hide our emotions in Texas."

Darrow looked over at me before starting the engine. "I wish things could be different."

"I understand. It must be very difficult."

Her forehead scrunched. "What do you mean?"

"With Caird."

"No, I wish things could be different with you and my brother. I really like you."

I smiled. "I really like you too."

As we pulled out of the gates of Whittaker Abbey, I felt the same regret I had earlier. It was unlikely I'd ever see it again.

"I'd invite you to the flat, but I wouldn't want to subject you to my mother."

"I have a great deal of work to do anyway."

"Right." Darrow pulled up in front of my hotel. "Maybe I could ring you when the duchess is finished lecturing me about whatever this week's topic might be."

"Yes," I answered absentmindedly. "We'll speak later." I closed the car door behind me and waved Darrow off.

I'd just walked through the courtyard of St. Ermin's and was about to go in through the revolving door of the hotel when my cell vibrated. Stupidly, I answered without checking who was calling.

"Are you finally back at the hotel, Harlow?" Sanborn spat when I accepted the call.

How did Sanborn know I hadn't been at the hotel, or how had she known where I was at all?

"You're going to miss your flight."

I looked at the clock in the lobby of the hotel. What time had the flight been scheduled for? "It's fine."

"Please. Don't lie to me, Harlow. I know you went above my head, and I don't like it one bit." Sanborn continued her expletive-laden rant, but I turned the volume down on the phone and held it away from my ear. The last words I heard clearly were, "I don't know what you're up to, but this isn't over."

I stared at the phone when the DHS officer ended the call. What did Sanborn know, other than I wasn't on the flight I'd been scheduled to be on, and why did she emphasize my name both times she'd said it?

Once in my room, the first thing I did was peel out of my clothes and get in the shower. Ten minutes later, I was dressed and ready to leave when my cell vibrated again.

If it was Sanborn calling a second time, I would let it go to voicemail. I didn't need the woman's shit, no matter what kind of cover I was trying to maintain. It wasn't her, though. The call was from a London number I didn't recognize.

"Harlow," I answered.

"Wren, it's Wilder."

"What is Caird's condition?" I asked, trying to keep my temper at bay and jumping straight into business mode.

"Critical. He's in the ICU at Thameside."

"I see."

"Listen—"

"I'm on my way." I ended the call before Wilder could protest. If he didn't want me to show up at the hospital, he shouldn't have told me that's where Caird was. He shouldn't have called me at all.

When my cell rang again, I considered turning it off. I looked at the screen, ready to reject the call but saw it was Leighton Marietta.

"Officer Harlow?"

"Yes, this is Wren."

"Agent Marietta here. I've been instructed by Agent Whittaker to meet you at St. Ermin's and take you to Thameside."

"That won't be necessary. I can get my own lift."

"I'm already here." The agent ended the call before I could protest, like I'd just done to Wilder.

When the elevator door opened, I saw the MI5 agent waiting for me in the lobby.

"I've been instructed to give you a new mobile and confiscate your other."

She tried to hand me a phone, but I refused to take it.

"You are being tracked," the agent said through gritted teeth. "And Caird did not attempt to kill himself."

I nodded and took the phone.

The agent led me through a door to the stairwell. Once we were one flight down, I took the sim card out of my government-issued cell, tossed the phone on the floor, and crushed it with my boot.

"We're pulling up now, sir," Marietta said, answering an incoming call a few minutes after we'd left St. Ermin's parking garage.

"Who was that?" I asked, more to see if the woman would tell me than wanting to know.

"The DG."

"Is all of MI5 at Thameside?"

"As is MI6."

I got out of the car when Agent Marietta pulled up to the door of the hospital, and entered the building through the revolving door. Once inside, I saw Wilder and Z waiting for me.

"You've met Z," said Wilder.

"Yes."

Z motioned for me to follow and led me to yet another stairwell, down several flights of stairs, and out a door into a parking garage that looked much like the one I'd just left.

"Where's Agent Whittaker?" I asked, noticing Wilder hadn't followed.

"He'll be meeting us at the next location," Z said, opening the passenger door of the only car on that level.

Before getting in, he put his arm around my shoulders. "What, no kiss hello?"

I stood on my toes and kissed his cheek.

"I've missed you, sweetheart."

"I've missed you too."

Z closed the door behind me and came around the other side. "Where are we going?" I asked.

"Where Matthew Caird really is."

13

Wilder

"Thanks," I said, climbing into George's waiting vehicle. "Did Harlow give you any trouble?"

George raised a brow and smirked. "For God's sake, Wilder, she's a DHS agent."

"Officer, but your point is?"

"She gave me no trouble."

"Her cell?"

"Destroyed."

"And her things?"

"Being delivered as we speak."

"I appreciate your help, George."

"It's my job, Whittaker."

Moments after Wren had ascended the stairs of my house without me last night, I received the first of a series of urgent messages.

Pinch arrived at my door five minutes later, and I left to meet with Shiver at the abbey.

An hour later, I returned to Dorchester House, greatly relieved when Pinch reported Wren had not come back downstairs nor did he hear any noise from her room.

I'd written the note, thanked Pinch a second time, and was walking out the door when I turned back around. "Hey, mate, be a bloke and make her some coffee in the morning."

"Bloody hell," I heard him mutter in a voice identical to Wellie's.

Whoever was tracking Wren already knew she was at Whittaker Abbey. It was best she stayed there until I could get everything set up in London.

Darrow had been an unwitting accomplice in delivering her to St. Ermin's before going to visit the duchess, where Rivet would brief her on what was going on. Or on as much of it as my sister needed to know.

"I'll be at headquarters if you need anything," said George when we arrived at the lowest level of the parking garage of the university hospital.

I got out of the car and waited there until Z arrived with Wren.

I opened her door and held out my hand, but she didn't take it. She looked between Z and me and folded her arms.

"When is either of you going to fill me in?"

"Soon, I promise," I answered, motioning to the lift.

"Is Caird here?" she asked Z.

"He is."

She didn't say anything more until after we exited on the tenth floor and I led her into a private room. Z waited in the hallway.

"Please take a seat. Can I get you anything?"

"I'll stand, and no, thank you." She folded her arms and leaned back against the wall.

"When did you last speak with anyone from DHS?"

"Why do you want to know?"

"Answer the question, Officer Harlow."

"Approximately ninety minutes ago."

"Whom with?"

"Amanda Sanborn."

I inwardly cringed. "Tell me about your conversation."

"Dammit, Whittaker. Quit interrogating me, and tell me what the hell is going on."

"Z received a call late last night from someone in your organization who has reason to believe you were being tracked by people not affiliated with your government or ours. This individual requested that you be taken to a secure location."

"What about Caird? Agent Marietta said it wasn't a suicide attempt."

I shook my head. "Someone tried to kill him and make it look as though he was attempting to take his own life."

"What evidence do you have?"

"Enough to be certain."

Wren dropped her arms and gripped the back of a chair. "That isn't the question I asked."

"I need to know more before I can answer your specific question."

"From whom?"

"You."

"I'm not saying another word until I speak with my contact directly."

"Of course," I answered, pushing the chair back in that I had just pulled out.

"Thank you."

I walked out of the room and into the hallway where Z was waiting.

"What's his condition?"

"No change."

It was ironic that in the last forty-eight hours I'd told Wren that if it had been up to me, Matthew would be dead. Now, I prayed the man would stay alive, if only long enough for us to find out who'd tried to kill him.

"The doctors think Caird was without air long enough for cerebral hypoxia to become anoxia."

"A reduced supply of oxygen that turned into total deprivation."

"That's correct."

"Brain damage is likely."

"Highly."

I ran my hand through my hair. "Have you notified Shiv?"

"I thought it best to leave that to you."

"What about Rivet?"

"On his way here now."

"And Darrow?"

"Pinch is responsible for securing your sister."

"Right," I mumbled. I knew what Z meant; I just wasn't crazy about the way he phrased it.

"Officer Harlow?"

"She requested to speak with 'her contact' privately."

Z nodded.

"Do you trust this person you're so secretive about, Z?" I asked.

"Whether I do or not is irrelevant."

"Unless Wren is in danger."

"The mobile is untraceable. No one but you will know where she is once she leaves here."

The door to the private room opened slightly. When Wren didn't come out, I went in and closed it behind me.

"Why am I in MI6 custody?"

I was confused. Where had that question come from? "You aren't."

"I'm to be taken to a secure location. Why isn't my own government facilitating it?"

"Because 'your contact,' as you called *her*, requested SIS handle it. Did she not explain that to you?"

"She informed me. She didn't explain. I want to know why."

"I can't answer on her behalf."

"What did you do?"

I pulled out a chair and motioned for her to be seated. Surprisingly, she did, so I sat in the chair beside her.

"I had nothing to do with it."

"Nothing at all?"

"I'm not sure what you're suggesting, Wren, but I'd hardly use the Secret Intelligence Service as a guise for keeping you in England, or whatever it is you're thinking."

"I requested immediate transport back to the States."

"And?"

"You already know her response, don't you, Whittaker?"

I hated the way she spat my name as though I had somehow become the enemy. "Tell me what you know, Wren."

"I don't know anything. My mission was to extradite Caird to the US."

"And investigate him."

"Not necessarily."

Her hostility puzzled me. "I'm not 'interrogating' you, Officer Harlow. I'm trying to figure out how best to protect you."

"I don't need to be protected."

"Your own government believes you do."

"Where am I being taken?"

"Somewhere safe."

Wren stood and folded her arms. "How serious is Caird's condition?"

"Very. The doctors think he may have suffered irreparable brain damage."

"Whether he lives or dies, they've succeeded in silencing him."

I studied her. There was something about her last statement that didn't sit right. Something was off. Her tone of voice had changed when she spoke, as did her expression. That, coupled with her hostile attitude, suddenly made sense.

"Who are you, Finley Harlow?"

"What do you mean?"

"What's your real mission?"

"I was sent to extradite Matthew Caird and return him to the United States to face prosecution."

"Evidently, the honesty you expect from me isn't to be reciprocated. Do you even work for DHS?"

I watched her closely. It had only been a split second, but I caught the quick intake of breath, the simultaneous eye movement. Would she even bother trying to lie to me?

"Why would you ask that question?"

"Why won't you answer?"

"Who I do or don't work for isn't relevant. I'm here on behalf of the United States government."

"NSA, then."

"I didn't say that."

I stood, rubbing the back of my neck. "You already know whom he was working with, don't you?"

She didn't need to respond; I could see the answer in her eyes.

I took a seat across from her and laid my arms out on the table. "Tell me this much, if nothing else."

She nodded, but with minimal movement of her head.

"Is my family in immediate danger?"

"I don't believe so."

Raising one arm, I slammed my fist down on the table. *"Yes or no."*

"I can't answer definitively."

"You've played this well, officer—or is it agent?"

I stood and walked out of the room; Z hadn't moved from where he stood earlier.

"Who does she work for?"

Z shook his head.

"Is she CIA or NSA?"

"I can't say for certain."

"Dammit, Z, don't make me fish. Tell me what you know."

"About what?" asked Shiver, coming around the corner.

"Come with me," Z said to us both.

"What about Harlow?" I asked.

"She isn't going anywhere," Z answered.

Given Caird was also on this floor, I should've known every entrance and exit was secure.

"Get me caught up," said Shiver as Z led us into another private meeting room and closed the door.

"Rivet is on his way up. He knows more than I do."

"We'll wait, then," said Shiver, squeezing my shoulder. "Give us a moment, Z?"

The DG nodded and left the room.

"You fill me in."

I told him about Wren's odd behavior. "I don't think she's with the DHS."

"Of course she isn't," said Shiver.

"What do you mean?"

"It was immediately obvious to me."

I stared him down. "It didn't occur to you to bloody tell me?"

"For God's sake, Wild, I figured you knew. Wasn't it part of your cat-and-mouse game with her?"

I pulled out a chair and sat down. "Z has never once let on whom his contact works for. I asked about Wren, and he said he couldn't say."

"What's your gut telling you?"

"NSA."

"Agreed."

"There's more, Shiv."

My brother sat down in the chair beside me.

"Wren knows whom Matthew was working with."

"She told you that?"

I shook my head. "No, but when I specifically asked, her reaction told me I was on the right track."

"That's why they asked Z to get her to a secure location."

"My guess is she knew coming in. Her mission was to get Matthew out of the UK. Rather than to interrogate him, it was to protect him," I speculated.

"And whomever they were protecting him from, got to him, so now Wren is in danger as well."

"It adds up, Shiv."

"What else did she say?" asked Shiver.

"She wants to return to the States, but the mystery woman pulling strings behind the scenes denied her request. When I told her I was merely trying to protect her, she told me she didn't need to be."

"Which, of course, means she does. Do you trust her, Wild?"

"Am I wrong to?"

Shiver shook his head. "No, you're not."

Rivet came in followed by Z and closed the door behind him.

"Before you begin, I'll accept nothing but the bloody truth from you, Riv," I told him.

"Matthew is dead." Rivet's voice caught.

"I'm sorry," I said at the same time I saw Shiver put his hand on Ranald's shoulder.

I stood and left the room. It didn't matter if Rivet knew whom Wren worked for. All I cared about was getting her out of here and somewhere safe. Once I did, I'd ask her again myself.

"What's happened?" Wren asked when I came back into the room where she was waiting.

"Caird is dead. We're leaving."

"Where are you taking me?"

"Somewhere you'll be safe."

I stalked toward her. Wren's back was against the wall, but that didn't mean she couldn't have moved. She didn't, even when I stood right in front of her and grasped the back of her neck with my hand.

"Shiver said he knew right away that you didn't work for DHS."

Wren looked into my eyes, but didn't respond.

"He also said that I was right to trust you."

I moved closer so my cheek rested against hers. "Tell me, Wren. Am I right to trust you?"

"Yes," she whispered.

"Do you trust me?"

"I do."

When I brushed her lips with mine, Wren put her arms around my waist. I wound my tongue around hers and put my hand on the small of her back, bringing her body closer to mine so her sex rested against my hardness.

"I'm only going to ask once. This, what's happening between us right now, is it what you want, Wren?"

"It is."

14

Wren

I watched as Wilder pulled out his cell phone, pushed a button on the screen, and brought it to his ear. "Meet us in the lowest level of the garage," he said and then disconnected the call.

He took my hand in his and led me out of the room and over to the elevator.

"Wilder?" I said when the door closed behind us and we were alone. "I'm sorry—"

"We're starting over, Finley Harlow. Whoever we were last night, isn't who we are today."

"What does that mean?"

"We'll discuss it once we're on our way."

When the elevator door opened to the garage, I saw Shiver waiting for us.

"Anything else we need to know before we leave?" Wilder asked his brother.

"Not at this time."

"Very well. You know where we'll be."

"I'll be in touch."

As we drove out of the garage, I saw Shiver was still standing near the bank of elevators.

"Is he okay?" I asked.

Wilder took my hand in his and brought it to his lips. "I'm not sure any of us are at the moment." He turned my hand over and kissed my palm. "But we will be."

We'd left the city and were on the motorway before either of us spoke again.

"Are you going to tell me where we're going?"

"Things are going to change between us, Wren, and for now, we're doing things my way."

"I guess that means no." I met his gaze before he turned back to look at the road. Where had the man gone who had kissed my hand only a few minutes earlier? "You said we're starting over and who we were last night isn't who we are today. You also said we'd discuss it once we were on our way. We're on our way."

Wilder scrubbed his face with his hand. "I'm taking you to Cumbria. My mother's parents were the Duke and Duchess of Cumberland. When they passed on, my uncle inherited the title and the estate. I'm his namesake."

"Uncle Sutton?"

I smiled when Wilder did. "Yes, but I can't quite imagine referring to him that way."

"What does Uncle Sutton think about my arrival?"

"*Our* arrival, and he isn't there. He also has a place in the South of France where he winters. The house is open for family members."

"He leaves it open?"

Wilder turned to me again, only this time, he was smiling rather than glaring. "Not literally. There are staff, Wren."

"Is he aware we're visiting?"

"He is."

"And does he know why?"

"We're on holiday."

"As a couple."

"That's right."

"Is that what you meant when you said things would be changing between us?"

Wilder grasped my hand like he had earlier. "When I asked specifically, you said you wanted it to happen, Wren. Have you changed your mind?"

"No."

"Good." He brought my palm back to his lips and kissed it. "I'm done denying either of us."

"What's going to happen, Wilder?" My own voice sounded breathy; my heart was ready to beat out of my chest, and the ache between my legs was maddening.

He let go of my hand. "Let me see you."

I raised a brow.

"Open your blouse, Wren. I want to look at you."

I was incredulous at what he was asking me to do; however, that didn't mean I wouldn't.

"Do it, Wren."

I slowly unfastened the buttons of my blouse.

"Spread it open and pull the cups of your bra out of my way."

My breath hitched as I opened it a minimal amount.

"Touch yourself."

"Wilder—"

"I didn't say you could talk. I told you to touch yourself."

The tone of his voice and his demands alone were almost enough to bring me to orgasm. God, how had he known I would respond to him the way I was?

"Do you want to know what I'm going to do to you when we get to Cumberland Manor?"

I couldn't speak.

"I'm going to kiss you. Everywhere. I'll touch you, and I'll look at you. Do you know how much I've longed to have you stand before me naked, just so I could look at you?"

"Wilder," I groaned, closing my eyes and taking a deep breath while I fought against covering myself.

"Maybe I'll send the staff away and then take your clothes so I can gaze at you as much as I like, and so you're naked and ready for me wherever and whenever I want you."

He reached over and moved my hand away from my breasts, putting his hand in its place. "Tell me what you're feeling."

Could I? Did I have the words to say that I'd never been more turned on in my life, never wanted a man more than I wanted him right now?

"Look at me."

I met his gaze.

"Tell me how your nipples feel."

"They're throbbing."

Wilder took a deep breath like I had moments before. "What else?"

"I want your hands on me."

"Just my hands?"

"No. I want everything."

"You have to tell me what you want, Wren. How else will I know?"

He was smiling, and before he returned his gaze to the road, he winked. How could he be so unaffected? A deep breath—was that all it took for him to get back under control? I felt like a pulsating puddle of need. I needed everything. His hands, his mouth, every part of him on me and inside me.

"Tell me now, Wren. You're running out of time," he said, cupping my sex with his hand.

"What do you mean?" I groaned.

"We're here, and once we're out of this car, it begins."

"Thank God," I breathed, moving to refasten my blouse.

"No," he said, taking one of my hands away. "Leave it."

"I can't just leave it open, Wilder. The staff…"

He pulled up to the gate and rolled down the window.

"Hello, sir," said a voice that came through an intercom.

"Good afternoon, Jarvis."

The gate opened, and Wilder pulled through, his hand still holding mine, keeping me from covering myself.

"Wilder, please…"

He pulled the car over and shut off the engine. "Not yet." He spread my blouse so it was completely open and brought his mouth to one nipple while he pinched the other with his fingertips.

My hands were in his hair, holding him where he was while, at the same time, wanting to push him away.

"I need you, Wilder. Don't make me wait any longer."

He nipped at the side of my breast and gave me a mercurial smile. "You'll wait, Wren. As long as I want you to."

How many people could Wilder's uncle possibly employ? Had they invited the neighbors over as well as everyone who lived in the nearby town? I felt as though I'd spent an hour shaking hands and thanking everyone who welcomed us and said to let them know if there was anything I needed.

Right now, all I needed was Wilder alone, naked, and preferably inside me. Every part of my body was at a heightened awareness. I could feel him breathe and his gaze as it settled on me. Where he moved, I followed.

I was right behind him when Wilder rounded a corner. He pushed me up against the wall and covered my now-hidden breasts with his hands.

"Please, Wilder…"

"What, my sweet? You still haven't told me what you want."

"Alone. Please, can we just be alone?"

"Soon, my precious little bird. Very soon."

Soon was nothing of the sort. When Jarvis, the man whose voice I'd heard at the gate, asked Wilder if he'd like afternoon tea served, the bastard agreed!

"You've got to be kidding," I said as he led me into a formal sitting room.

"What's wrong?" he asked, cupping my cheek.

I was tempted to swat it away. However, at the same time he brought his lips to mine, he reached between my legs.

"What do you want, Wren?"

"Sex," I gasped as he tightened his hold on me.

He pulled back and looked into my eyes. "Are you sure? Maybe you'd like to think about it a while longer."

"No. I don't want to do any more thinking. I need you inside me, Wilder. Now."

He smirked. "But Jarvis is bringing us tea."

"You have two choices, Whittaker. You can take me upstairs or wherever the closest bedroom is and we can do this in private, or we can remain here and Jarvis will share in your first glimpse of me completely naked."

"I see. Well, I'm not sure the bloke's heart could take it," he murmured. He took my hand, led me from the sitting room, and up the grand staircase I'd seen when we came in.

By the time we reached a closed door, I was ready to rip Wilder's clothes from his body. Instead, I began removing mine.

We went into a bedroom, and as he watched, I unbuttoned my blouse and slid it off my shoulders. I reached behind to unfasten my bra.

"Trousers first," he said, coming and kneeling in front of me. He moved my hands away and unfastened my belt, then the button, and finally, the zipper. Wilder reached behind and grabbed my bottom with both of his hands. He yanked my pants down and over my hips. When I tried to lower my panties, he swatted my hands away.

"Shoes." He unzipped my ankle boots and slowly took each one off. "Step out," he said, removing my pants from around my ankles. "I want to see you like this. Get on the bed, Wren."

I rested my head on the pillows and watched as he slowly spread my legs and came to kneel between them. He ran his finger over the lace of my black panties.

"I like this," he said, fingering the bright-pink bow that rested just above my pulsating sex. "And this," he said, reaching up to tug on the same color bow on my bra.

With one hand, he kneaded my breast, while with the other, he snaked two fingers under the black lace and into my wetness.

When his mouth followed his fingers, I felt as though my body would split apart.

"I need to see you," I begged, pulling at his shirt.

Wilder stood and removed it, tossing it in the same pile where my clothes had landed. He unzipped his pants and let them fall to his feet.

I raised a brow and smiled. "Commando?"

"Always."

My eyes ran the length of his now-naked body, wondering how in the world I was going to accommodate him.

"Please, God, tell me you have a condom," I groaned.

Wilder picked up the same pants he'd just tossed aside and pulled one out of his pocket.

"Is that the only one you have?" I whined.

He smiled. "Not by a long shot, darling."

I was mesmerized by the way he moved. My eyes trailed from his hardness, up his ridiculously ripped torso.

"Take off the bra first and then the knickers," he demanded as he rolled on the condom. He got back on the bed, resting between my legs.

"You are magnificent," he muttered, running his hands from my shoulders, toying with my nipples, fingertips grazing my ticklish tummy, until finally, finally he rested against me.

"Put me inside of you," he said, gasping as I reached for him. "Now, Wren," he demanded when my hands took too long exploring.

"Legs around me." He moved just slightly, and I moaned.

"Give me a second," I said.

"One thousand and one," he said, thrusting hard into me.

My body arched, and my heels dug into his back while my fingers did the same to his shoulders.

Wilder wrapped my long red hair around his hand and held tight as his motions went from slow and calculated to fast, hard, and frenzied.

As his body thrust into mine, his mouth devoured my mouth.

"More," I begged, and he rocked forward until his body was flush against me. Somewhere in the back of my mind, I could feel his hands as they grasped my bottom, holding me still as he jackhammered into me.

"Wilder…God…I can't…" I could barely speak. He'd kept me on the edge for so long, and now I felt the climax barreling through me.

"Wait," he said as I clenched around him.

"I can't…"

He moved his hips and surged into me. *"Now."*

I'd never been a screamer, until today. Over and over, I screamed his name as I writhed and rode the pleasure his body was delivering to mine.

"We aren't done," he said, rolling until I was on top of him.

"I can't," I repeated for the third time.

"You can," he said, standing and walking over to the wall with me wrapped around him. My arms were tight around his neck as he pounded into me, using the full force of his powerful legs.

He impaled me, giving me one final thrust before he made me take all of him. He buried his head in my neck, licking the moisture from my skin as I felt him explode inside me. I clung to him as he carried me back over to the bed.

"Don't move," he said as he went into the adjoining bath to dispose of the condom.

When he came back, I was attempting to crawl under the blankets.

"Are you cold?"

"Not yet," I said, still trying to slow my breathing, "but I will be."

"No, my sweet Wren. You will not."

When he covered my body with his, I knew he intended to keep mine well heated.

15

Wilder

Once I was certain Wren was asleep, I crawled out from next to her. Logs were stacked in the fireplace, so all I had to do was light the kindling, and soon it would be roaring.

I walked over to the door, delighted to see that someone had delivered our bags. I brought them in, unzipped an outer pocket, and put the package of condoms in the drawer of the bedside table. I may have been overly optimistic, but my every instinct screamed that Wren wanted me as much as I wanted her, so I'd packed them.

While it had been a much longer stretch without sex than I was accustomed to, it wasn't just abstinence that drove my body to take hers in the way I had.

It was so much more. It was her. Our bodies fit as though God had made them two perfect pieces of a puzzle. Her cries drove me on, building my need while quenching my desire. Even now, as she'd just drifted to sleep, I craved more from her.

I studied her delicate features. She looked so peaceful and not the slightest bit stressed as she had since the day she'd first walked into my office. Had it been days? Not a week. Not even seventy-two hours, and yet, I felt as though I'd known Finley "Wren" Harlow for most of my life.

Earlier, I'd expected to feel anger when I realized she hadn't been honest about whom she really worked for. Even that she knew whom Matthew had been working with, hadn't driven me to rage. Instead, the only time I'd felt myself hovering near the breaking point was when she didn't confirm or deny whether my family was in danger.

For now, it was up to Shiver and Pinch to make sure they weren't. Rivet too. My only concern was the woman who turned her body in her sleep and reached for me. I drew her onto my chest, and she snuggled against me. "Wilder," she murmured.

I ran the fingertips of one hand over the soft skin of her back while I covered her breast with the other. I was serious about not letting her prevent me from having constant access to her body.

I had no idea what she'd expected from me. Perhaps she'd decided that no Englishman could take her body in a way it never had been before, but she couldn't be more wrong. I'd push her every limit, bring her to heights of pleasure she didn't know existed. When I said we were just getting started, I meant it.

Wren rolled over so her back was to my front. I nestled my hardness between the cheeks of her luscious bottom and snaked my hand around to cup her sex.

She moaned and writhed when I put two fingers inside her wetness. She was as ready for me as I was for her.

I woke at dawn and smiled, looking at the beautiful creature in bed beside me.

I'd taken her again and again throughout the night; each time her passion rose to mine.

I wondered what she'd say, how she'd react, if I made good on my promise not to allow her to dress today. Would she balk, or would it excite her?

Intuitively, I knew that Wren would respond best if I took charge and gave her limited choices. Regardless of whom she worked for, she was a badass, take-charge, get-the-job-done professional. When I demanded she relinquish control, though, I could feel her arousal surge.

Today I planned to get to know every inch of her body by daylight. I'd instructed Jarvis to have food and drink delivered outside the bedroom door so we didn't have to leave its confines.

When there was the faintest knock at the door, I wasn't certain if I imagined it. When I heard it again, I eased Wren off my arm, got out of bed, and pulled on my trousers. I opened the door to find a cart like one might see in a hotel, laden with coffee, tea, assorted breakfast pastries, and fruit. I wheeled it inside and saw Wren sitting up in bed, the sheet pulled up to just below her chin.

"Drop it," I said, closing the door behind me.

She grinned and pulled it higher.

"You're going to regret that, my sweet little bird."

She squealed when I stalked to the bed and pulled the sheet from her hands. I lay beside her and buried my face between her breasts, rewarded with the glorious sound of Wren's giggles.

"Stop," she said, pushing me away. "I smell coffee. I need coffee."

"You Yanks and your coffee," I winked, getting up to pour her a cup. I added cream and handed it to her.

"How did you know?"

"What's that?" I asked, unfastening my trousers, letting them drop to the floor, and joining her on the bed.

"Cream. No sugar."

"I'll never tell."

"Oh my God," she groaned as she took a sip. "For a country that consumes twenty times more tea than coffee, you sure do it well."

"It's the French influence."

"I don't care what it is. It's divine."

I stood, poured myself a cup of tea, set it on the bedside table, and made Wren a plate of food.

"I could get used to the view from here," she murmured. When I turned around, I found her looking at my backside rather than out the window.

"Me too." I pulled the sheet all the way from her body and handed her the plate of pastries and fruit.

She broke off a piece of croissant and popped it into her mouth, followed by a strawberry. My mouth watered with want to taste her as much as the fruit.

Wren set the plate on the table near her side of the bed and pulled her knees up to her chin.

"We need to talk."

I took a sip of tea and put it on my side table. "We don't. Not if you aren't ready."

"I am, and I do want you to know that I'm sorry I wasn't honest with you about who I work for."

"You must have had your reasons."

"I wasn't honest about why I was really in England either."

"I'm aware."

"I've managed to fly well under the radar since the start of my career. Those days, I fear, are over. Whoever tried to kill—killed—Caird, may know who I am and why I'm in the UK."

"To extradite Caird."

"Yes, that was my plan. However, it was only as a matter of convenience in order to allow me to maintain my cover as an officer of the US Department of Homeland Security."

I raised a brow. By her body language alone, I knew she was lying. Why, when she was confessing everything else?

"You have heard, I'm sure, of the Five Eyes."

I shifted my weight off my arm and sat up, suddenly feeling as though I should put my clothes on.

"*Jesus.* You work for Vera."

Wren nodded.

Amelia "Vera" Watkins was the current and first female head of National Centre for Geospatial Intelligence—one of the "Five Eyes" Wren referenced. Formally known as the Allied System for Geospatial Intelligence, or ASG, the organization's other four members were the Australian Geospatial-Intelligence Organisation, the Canadian Forces Intelligence Command, GEOINT New Zealand, and the UK's own, National Centre for Geospatial Intelligence.

Vera, Z's mystery contact, was considered to be among the most powerful women in worldwide intelligence.

"I'm curious…"

"Go ahead."

"How does Z rate direct access to Watkins?"

Wren threw her head back and laughed. "Of all the questions you could've asked."

"Does he know who she is?"

"Yes."

"What about Sanborn? Who is she to you?"

Wren rolled her eyes. "Amanda Sanborn believes she is my boss."

I struggled not to laugh to the point where I found it necessary to cover my mouth with my hand.

"By the way, I've subsequently been briefed on what happened between the two of you."

The smile left my face. "How? Never mind. That's the kind of question my sister would ask."

"I'm sorry I wasn't honest with you, Wilder, but I needed you to believe I was who you were told I was."

While I understood, I didn't like it. In fact, I was beginning to feel very well-played indeed. I stood, put on not only my trousers, but my shirt as well. Wren, however, stayed right where she was, not even pulling the sheet up to cover herself.

"I don't know much," she backtracked. "Only that she was smitten."

"That's one word for it."

Wren held out her hand, but I didn't take it.

How could I describe to her the way I felt when I didn't understand it myself?

Emasculated? Yes.

Foolish? Definitely.

As I had in my office when Z proposed George take over my job at MI5, I was stunned that all this time, I'd believed I had the upper hand with Miss Harlow. I couldn't have been more wrong.

"Wilder?"

My back was to her, and I wasn't certain I could bring myself to turn around. When I didn't, I heard her padding toward me. She stood before me, naked as she had been since last night.

"Please don't tell me that I shouldn't have confided in you."

"Why did you?"

"Was I here alone last night?"

I looked into her eyes "What do you mean?"

"That may have been standard operating procedure for you, Whittaker, but it wasn't for me. I've never, ever experienced the pleasure you gave me. I can't imagine that anyone else could ever satisfy me again. It isn't just that, Wilder. I felt a connection. Was I wrong?"

I studied her eyes, the expression on her face. Was she playing me further? I didn't think so, but I never would've guessed whom she really worked for either.

"I need time."

"Why?" she asked, taking a step back and covering herself with a throw that had been at the end of the bed.

I struggled with how to respond. "You've cut me off a bit at my knickers."

Wren shook her head. "Wow. Really? I don't think I've ever been so disappointed in my life. I thought you were…so much more." I watched as she grabbed her clothes, but instead of putting them on, she spun around and glared at me. "You said you needed time. Go." She turned her back.

I stood my ground. I didn't want to stay, but I didn't want to leave either. Hadn't I told myself that Wren was as badass as they came? Yet she'd responded to me in a way that assured me, without any question, she wanted me to take charge. She hadn't been the aggressor once, with the exception of when she'd threatened to bare her body to Jarvis.

She hadn't hesitated with anything I'd ask of her once she got over her initial surprise when I demanded she expose the breasts I longed to touch at this moment.

This was it, the moment of reckoning. Whatever I chose to do in the next few seconds would determine how it would be between us from now on.

"No, I bloody won't go," I growled, taking her by the shoulders and spinning her around to face me. There was nothing I could say that would undo the damage I'd done in the last few minutes, but there was plenty I could do with my body.

I wrenched the clothes from her hands and tossed them across the room. The throw landed in the same pile. I pinned her hands behind her back with one hand while I grasped the back of her neck with the other.

I was close enough to kiss her, but I wouldn't. "One more time, Wren. Tell me this is what you want."

"More than anything."

16

Wren

There wasn't a single place on my body that didn't ache, but if Wilder asked to do it all again, I wouldn't hesitate. He knew exactly how far to push me without going over the edge into something that wouldn't excite me.

I had no interest in being tied up or spanked or any of the other creepy things people seemed obsessed with as of late.

But Wilder got it. He demanded things of me, but all for my own pleasure. He was the most unselfish lover I'd ever been with. He drove me hard and then was so gentle it almost brought me to tears.

I'd been afraid he was going to walk out on me earlier. If he had, I would've been devastated. I'd let my guard down, let him in, even told him whom I worked for. If he had walked away then, I knew I'd never trust any man again.

We still had a lot to talk about. There was more I needed to tell him, but now wasn't the right time.

In fact, until Wilder brought it up, I wouldn't say another word.

I looked down and saw his eyes were open and he was studying me.

"You've worn me out, lass," he said, reaching up to tweak my exposed nipple. Even that sent pleasure surging through my body.

"Wilder...I..."

He leaned up, resting on his elbow. "Out with it."

"You're amazing."

He smiled, but then scrunched his eyes. "What were you going to say before you talked yourself out of it?"

"Thank you for bringing me here. I'm not the kind of person who accepts help easily."

"You're welcome, and like I said to you once before—in a time and place that feels years ago—I'm honored that you trust me."

"It's getting dark." I looked out the window, stunned that we'd spent the entire day in bed with the exception of the multiple times we'd lounged in the adjoining bath's oversized tub.

"Are you anxious to get out of this room?" he asked.

"Not really."

"Good. Neither am I. Are you bored, though?"

I laughed. "You can't be serious. Bored? I can't imagine ever being bored when I'm with you."

His cheeks flushed, which I found adorable.

"Are you hungry?"

I rubbed my stomach. It seemed as though food was delivered to our room on the hour. "I don't think I'll eat again for a week."

"Nah," he said, grasping the back of my neck and bringing his lips to mine. "I need you well nourished."

He sat up and put his arm around my shoulders, pulling me to him so my head rested against his chest. "What is troubling you, my sweet Wren?"

I'd vowed I wouldn't tell him the rest until I had to. I'd already said too much. He was beginning to matter, and if that happened, I'd no longer be in control of the situation. There weren't many times in my life when I hadn't had the upper hand. With men, my career, even school.

From elementary school on, I'd always been the brightest, smartest student in the room. It continued until I graduated from college, when I met "Vera," on the same day I got my diploma.

***

"Kennedy?" I heard a woman's voice say. It sounded so much like my mother, I spun around to face a woman who didn't look the slightest bit familiar.

"I'm sorry, did I startle you?" she asked.

"No. It's just that your voice…you sounded like my mother." I fought against threatening tears. The last thing I'd do is cry in front of a stranger.

"I'm so sorry. Especially on a day like today. I'm sure you miss her very much."

"Who are you?" I asked, taking a step back. How did this woman know anything about my life?

"My name is Amelia Watkins." She held out her hand, and I shook it. "I've had my eye on you."

I didn't need to ask why. While I hadn't recognized her, there wasn't a woman or man in my field of study who wouldn't know the name.

"Thank you, ma'am," I said, feeling almost as though I should curtsy.

The woman pulled a card out of her pocket and handed it to me. "I'm sure you want to enjoy your evening with your father and brother, celebrating your extraordinary achievements. Call me Monday, and we'll chat."

"Yes, ma'am," I said, watching the woman walk away.

There hadn't been a single professor, class, or exam that made me as nervous as Amelia Watkins had. I was so ornery in the time between my graduation and Monday morning, that my father and brother threatened to return to Texas.

"I'm sorry, please don't leave," I'd begged, only to realize they were teasing me.

"I've never seen anyone rattle you the way this woman has," my father said. "Remember who you are and that she came to you."

***

"Where have you gone off to?" asked Wilder, running his finger down my cheek.

"I was just thinking about the first time I met Vera."

"Is it a good story? I don't think I've ever met anyone who is as good a storyteller as you are."

"This one isn't that interesting. She came to my graduation from the University of Virginia."

"Was she a speaker?"

"Actually, no. I don't know why she was there. And I never asked." I shook my head. "Three days later, she offered me a job. I've worked for her ever since."

"She's quite…formidable."

I laughed. "Perfect word. She's also brilliant."

"Sounds like someone else I've recently had the pleasure of meeting."

"Thank you, but I'm not on her level."

"Don't sell yourself short. There was a reason she snapped you up before anyone else had the chance."

"She's my mentor."

"It's important to her that you're safe."

I shivered and pulled the blanket over me.

"I'll relight the fire," Wilder said, rolling off the bed and walking over to the fireplace.

The man in clothes was swoon-worthy. Naked, he was godlike. He bent down to add wood to the fire, tossed kindling on the bigger logs, and struck the match.

"Where did you learn to build a fire?"

"Uh-oh, not up to Texas standards?" he asked, stretching his body out next to mine.

"Not at all, actually. You're very good at it."

"Wellie. Like most everything else I learned as a child."

"Pinch's father?"

"That's right."

"I wish I could've met him."

Wilder brushed a wisp of hair from my face. "You will. I'll make sure of it the next time we're at the abbey."

"I thought…"

Wilder brushed my bottom lip with his finger, leaned forward, and kissed me. "Tell me," he said, the demanding tone back in his voice, the one that set my blood on fire.

"I didn't think I'd be back."

"Why ever not?" he asked, backing away to look into my eyes.

"Your note. I thought you were avoiding me."

"Wait. The note I left when I had to go to London?"

I nodded.

"I wrote that it was an urgent matter."

I looked away when I felt my cheeks heat, wishing I'd kept my mouth shut.

"Look at me, Wren."

Lying side by side, I could see the confusion on Wilder's face as his eyes searched mine for answers.

"I asked you to come to bed."

Wilder shook his head. "You didn't."

"All but."

He cupped my face with his palm. "I'd very much like you to come back to Whittaker Abbey. In fact, it would please me if you became a regular visitor. Although, I can't promise you'll spend much time with Wellie or anyone else other than me."

"Darrow will be disappointed."

"Yes." He sighed. "My sister has claimed you as her best mate."

"Are you unhappy about that?"

"Not at all."

I raised a brow.

"You have a brother."

"Yes, but I don't see what—"

"Imagine you also had a best friend who lived on your family's ranch, someone you spent countless hours with when you were a child. Even as an adult."

"I'm with you."

"You find out that your brother and this imaginary best friend are seeing each other."

"That they kept it a secret would bother me the most."

"Not me. I would have been more than happy to remain in the dark for perpetuity."

"Why?"

"I grew up with Pinch. Let's just say adolescent boys…talk."

"Have you told them how you feel?"

Wilder sighed and looked up at the ceiling. "We're all in our thirties at this point. Is it really any of my business?"

"She cares a great deal for him, and it seems mutual."

"Did she tell you that?"

"No, but at dinner…it seemed…"

"That's my worry. Pinch Fulton has never been known to be monogamous."

"Like you."

"Touché."

Wilder put his arms around me and rolled us both so I was on top of him. He put his hands on either side of my face and kissed me.

"You'll think I'm daft," he said, looking into my eyes, "and you may even doubt I'm telling you the truth, but until you, I've never met a woman who I wanted to be monogamous with."

Part of me wanted to hear him say it again. I wanted him to reassure me that he didn't say that to everyone, but it would be far too humiliating.

"Tell me, Wren." He brushed the hair from my face a second time. "Am I worthy of your monogamy?"

I tried to roll away, but he held tight.

"Answer me."

"Yes," I whispered.

He rolled us both then, so his body rested on mine. "Are you sore?"

"Everywhere."

"I see," he said.

Wilder scooted his body down mine until his mouth was where he could lave my soreness away.

17

Wilder

On Monday, we forced ourselves out of bed and downstairs for breakfast, although Wren said she wished she didn't have to face the staff, who knew where we'd spent the last thirty-six hours and why.

It reminded me that I'd meant to shoo Jarvis and the rest of the household away, so I could keep Wren naked all day and night.

"Oh, no," she said when I looked up at her.

"What?"

"I know that look, and you promised me a tour of the estate this morning."

I laughed. "I shall keep my promise. In fact, I was thinking we could ride this afternoon."

Wren cringed.

"Not a good idea?"

She squirmed in her chair. "Maybe tomorrow."

I laughed again and reached across the table to run my thumb over the back of her hand. "I won't apologize."

"I didn't expect you to." The expression on her face turned from playful to worried.

"What's that look about?" I asked.

"Life, and while I would love to keep the rest of the world at bay for a little while longer, there are things happening that I need to deal with. Have you received any updates?"

"Nothing yet, but I expect I'll hear from Shiver today."

"Does anyone know where I am?"

I smiled. "Did you think we could hide you from Vera?"

Wren smiled too. "I'd feel better if I could speak with her."

"Again?"

"What do you mean? I haven't spoken with her since I left the States."

"What about when we were at the hospital?"

Wren cringed like she had a moment ago. "I had to check in with Sanborn. For all intents and purposes, I am a junior officer at DHS."

"Why? I mean, isn't it common knowledge that you work for the NGA?"

Wren looked away. "Finley Harlow doesn't work for the NGA."

"I see."

I stood, letting the ramifications of what she'd just said sink in.

"Evidently, the supposed connection you felt wasn't enough for you to tell me your real name." I was headed out of the room when she asked me to wait.

"It's Kennedy. Kennedy King."

I put a hand against the wall and leaned my full weight on my arm. If I hadn't, I might've had to sit down.

"Wren?"

"It's what my father called me."

"You *have* flown under the radar."

She stood and walked over to the window. "Can I ask you something?"

"Of course."

"Did Shiver really think Losha would be able to walk away from United Russia easily?"

I didn't know all the details, but what I'd been told was that Shiver's now wife, Orina "Losha" Kuznetsov, had, at one time, a multimillion-dollar bounty on her head, in part, because she hadn't fulfilled her mission to kill my older brother. The bounty had been lifted as part of a deal pieced together primarily by the CIA, in which United Russia, the modern-day equivalent of the KGB as well as the ruling political party, walked away with a sum purported to be in the billions. Of course, Losha's bounty being lifted had only been a fraction of what the US got in exchange. I wasn't sure what this had to do with Caird or with Wren's real name.

"Does Shiver know who you are?"

"If you had stayed, you would've known too."

"Rivet briefed him?"

"My assumption is that Vera briefed him between the time the prison guards found Matthew and he died."

"Where is my brother and his family now?"

"I don't know, Wilder, but I'm sure they're somewhere safe."

"Why didn't you just return to the US? That would've been the logical thing to do in order to maintain your cover."

"I did."

"I don't understand."

"If anyone were to check, Finley Harlow boarded a flight Saturday morning out of Heathrow."

"Only you were being tracked, so someone knew you were at Whittaker Abbey and not on that plane."

"Any guesses who?" she asked with a sneer.

"Sanborn?"

"Bingo. What I don't know is whether she's a whack-job control freak who wanted to know if I had sex with you, or if she's associated with any foreign intelligence agencies."

"Where is Sanborn now?"

"Remember, this is all speculation on my part since I haven't been able to talk to anyone in Washington, but I would think she's being interrogated."

"In order to find out if she has any idea who you really are."

Wren walked over and stood in front of me. Just being in her presence put me on the hit list of at least ten countries I could name off the top of my head.

"My job, then, is to keep you well hidden until Vera determines whether your cover has been compromised."

She put her hand on my arm. "I hope you understand that I have chosen to trust you with a secret almost no one in the world knows."

This wasn't like before, when I'd felt emasculated because Wren told me she worked for the NGA. No, this was on an exponentially higher level. The woman who stood before me, the one I originally thought of as "cute," was Kennedy King. The name was spoken in awed whispers by many who believed she was a composite of several people in US intelligence rather than a single person. *Jesus,* I couldn't even wrap my head around the fact that I was in her presence.

"Here's what I don't get. Why, in the name of God, after knowing me for barely seventy-two hours, would you divulge a secret that the intelligence world has kept for ten or more years?"

Wren got close enough that I could feel her breath on my neck. "I know everything about you; I just hadn't met you yet. I figured you deserved the same."

I walked out of the room, praying she wouldn't follow. I'd said I needed time before, but now I really meant it. The one person I would immediately go to with this was, according to Wren, in hiding as much as we were. I went outside, pulled my mobile out of my pocket, and called Shiver's mobile anyway.

I almost wretched when I got a recording that the number was no longer in service. Frantically, I called Pinch and then Darrow and got the same message for both of them. I didn't dare call Wellie. I knew better, and if I'd had my wits about me fifteen seconds ago, I wouldn't have called Darrow either.

"Sutton," I heard a familiar voice say, and turned to see Z walking toward me.

My gut reaction was to reach for my gun, but I'd just walked away from an hours-long sex marathon and hadn't considered needing to be armed for breakfast.

"Why are you here?"

"I've been nearby, along with a number of other agents."

"I thought you said no one would know where she was but me."

"Now that you know who she is, you also know why I couldn't tell you the truth."

"How do you know I know?"

"She has an emergency button on her phone. Several, in fact. Each to alert us of varying degrees of danger."

"Was there one specifically for me?"

Z didn't respond, but I laughed anyway.

"Do you know I asked her how you rated a direct connection to Vera?"

"I have a name, Wilder," I heard Wren say from behind me.

"Right. Finley Kennedy Wren Harlow King. It's hard to know which to use."

"You aren't a child, Sutton; quit behaving like one," said Z.

"I'm leaving." I went back into the house and upstairs to get the keys to my car. Along the way, I didn't see a single member of my uncle's staff. As I turned to leave—gun, keys, and identification in hand—Wren was standing in the doorway.

"You know you can't go anywhere."

"Bloody hell I can't."

"They'll stop you."

"Are you saying the DG of MI5 is going to shoot me?"

"If it came down to that."

I sat on the bed and put my head in my hands.

Wren walked over. "You asked me why, after knowing you such a short amount of time, I trusted you with my secret."

"I bloody know now, don't I? Because I'm fucking expendable. God, I'm such an idiot."

When I looked up, Wren was no longer in front of me. She wasn't even in the room.

18

Wren

"I warned you," said Z when I came downstairs.

"What is the expression you Brits use? Sod off?"

"We're just as apt to say fuck off."

"Then fuck off, Z."

"Wren," he said with a far too paternal tone in his voice.

"Don't do that."

"Just because you refuse to call me by the honorific, doesn't make me any less your father."

He walked over and put his arm around me, pulling me close. I rested my head on his shoulder and let myself cry.

He'd warned me, and I was an idiot. People like me didn't meet someone and fall in love. "What do you think he'll do?"

"The same thing you'd do. I wouldn't have let it get this far if I believed otherwise."

"I thought he was different."

"I know," said my father, stroking my hair.

"Now what?"

"Now there's one more person in the world who knows who you really are, and he won't tell a soul."

"We have to leave."

Z shook his head. "No one is going anywhere until we know where we stand."

"Any word?"

"Not yet, but you've met Sanborn. Do you really think she's good enough to fool you?"

I shook my head.

"Go lie down and get some rest."

"Where?"

"The same place you slept last night."

I watched my father walk out the front door of Wilder's uncle's house, wondering if he was crazy or if I should do as he said.

I slowly ascended the staircase, like I had at Wilder's house, alone. Had he left through some other exit I knew nothing about?

I crept down the hallway and peered into the bedroom where I'd experienced the most incredible sex of my life, but more importantly, as I'd told him, the first real connection I'd ever felt.

Wilder was sitting on the edge of the bed, exactly where he'd been when I went downstairs.

"No more lies," he spat without looking at me.

I walked closer.

"Who is he to you?"

"Who are you talking about?"

"Z."

I sat down next to him. I'd never told anyone most of the things I'd told Wilder in the span of a few hours. "He's my father."

"Holy Mother of God," he groaned. "Do you know he…never mind. His last name is Alexander. Yours is King."

"Kennedy King Alexander is how my birth certificate reads. Not that anyone could ever get their hands on a copy of it."

Wilder turned and faced me. "When I was telling you about my sister and Pinch, you said the lie would be what bothered you the most."

"And you said you would've preferred not to know."

"What else is there…I don't know what to call you."

"Wren. Call me Wren like you've been doing. It's my name."

"Okay, Wren, what else is there? Because I'm telling you that if you say in two hours that Vera is really your mother, I'll lose it."

"My mother is dead. That isn't a lie."

"I'm sorry for that." He reached over and brushed a tear from beneath my eye, one I hadn't realized I'd shed.

"Why me?" he asked.

I scooted back on the bed so I was resting against the pillows. Longing for the closeness we'd felt before, I reached my hand out to him.

"I'll answer you," I said when, to my surprise, he came to lie next to me. "But first I have a question for you."

He studied me.

"I've told you everything about me, Wilder. Tell me one thing about yourself. Answer my question."

"Okay." He kept his eyes on me; he didn't look or shrink away.

"Why me?"

He went so long before answering, just staring into my eyes, that I began to doubt he would.

"It isn't a short answer," he finally said.

"Neither of us is going anywhere."

He didn't laugh or smile; he just continued staring into my eyes.

"The reason I'm taking so long to answer, Wren, is because these are things I haven't begun to admit to myself."

My first inclination was to move away from him, but since he didn't, I stayed still.

"I knew the minute you waltzed into my office that I couldn't let you go. I've never felt that way before." When he cupped my cheek with his palm, I felt as though I might melt with relief.

"First of all, and I'm sorry for being a typical man, but you're magnificent."

I raised a brow.

"You're gorgeous and you know it."

"I've always been a bit of a tomboy."

Wilder rested one hand on my breast. "No, sweetheart, there's nothing boy about you." He left his hand where it was, and I covered it with mine. There was no better feeling in the world than having his hands on me again.

"I have an idea," he said, taking his hand away and sitting up. "I don't know about you, but I'm feeling really naked at the moment, like I'm about to expose myself to the world."

"Yeah, I feel that way."

"So let's really go for it. Clothes off, secrets exposed, feelings revealed, all of it."

"Are you serious?"

Wilder's expression changed as did his voice. "Let me see you."

I hesitated. Could I open myself up more than I had?

"Now, Wren."

I stood. My hands were shaking as I unfastened my blouse and let it fall from my shoulders. I waited for him to do the same. He only fussed with one button before pulling the shirt off over his head. Then he put his hands on his hips.

Because he'd told me before that he wanted me to take my pants off before my bra, that's what I did now. I removed my boots and socks, and stepped out of them.

Wilder took off his shoes and socks.

"That isn't fair. Take your pants off."

"Two things. First, you know better than to use that tone with me. Second, once my trousers are off, I will be completely naked, as you know." He motioned for me to remove my bra.

I unfastened it and let it fall to the floor.

We stood, staring into each other's eyes. I wiggled out of my panties at the same time he let his pants drop. He held out his hand, and I took it.

"You're shaking," he said, bringing it to his lips.

"Since we're exposing secrets, I'll admit I'm terrified."

He led me over to the bed. "Of?"

We lay down, side by side, and faced each other. My eyes filled with tears.

"Tell me why you're terrified, Wren."

I took a deep breath.

"Say it."

"You first."

"No. Say it," he repeated.

"I'm terrified that you're not going to want me."

Wilder smiled. "That isn't what you were going to say, but that's an easy one. Take one look at me, and you'll know exactly how much I want you."

I'd already noticed.

"Fair is fair. Plus, it was my turn anyway. So I'll tell you. I'll warn you that the words aren't going to be flowery or romantic. I haven't had time to prepare."

"I just want to hear how you feel."

"I've already told you that you're absolutely gorgeous, and when you sat your luscious arse on the edge of my desk, I almost slammed the door on poor Mrs. Udele, and ravished you there and then."

"I felt the same way."

"When I leaned forward and almost touched you?"

"Yes," I whispered.

"Next, I suppose, was your wit. You're quick and I loved that."

"Keep going."

"You're smart. No, that's not right. You're bloody brilliant. You drink bourbon. You're funny, did I already say that?"

"You did."

"Don't interrupt me; I'm on a roll. You are so badass, but in the car, the way you responded to me. It was so perfect."

"Do all—"

Wilder put his fingertips on my lips. "We are talking about you and me. No one else. Understood?"

"Okay."

"What were the words you used? Standard operating procedure? No. I assure you I've never come close to feeling the way I do when I'm with you. Everything about you excites me. *Everything.*"

"Even knowing who I really am?"

"Bloody hell, don't get me started on that. You have no idea all the questions I want to ask that I know you can never answer." He went from smiling to serious. "Your turn, Wren. Why me?"

"You're the only man I've ever met who I believed was strong enough not to walk away."

"You knew that right off?"

I shook my head. "At first I thought it would just be, you know, sex. But then, Sanborn."

"You know I was never with her, right? I swear it."

"Yes. I got it. Seriously, though. I told you before that I knew everything about you."

"Yes," he said, grinning.

"But there was a part of me that hoped, once I got to know you, I wouldn't be as attracted."

"How did that work out for you?"

I swatted at him, and he kissed me.

"Z—my father—warned me."

"Don't get me started on that either. My God, I don't want to think about the conversations he and I had."

"Wilder?"

"Yes, Wren?"

"Why are you being like this? You were so angry."

"I already told you why."

"Tell me again."

"I knew the minute I met you, I couldn't let you go."

"And now?"

"Nothing has changed."

We lay together, just like that, for so long that I lost track of time. Before I knew it, it was getting dark.

"I'll light a fire," he said when I shivered.

I watched as I had the night before, loving the way his body moved.

"I have more questions," he said, crawling back up on the bed.

"Okay."

"What happens next?"

"Z is waiting for word from Washington. Neither of us thinks Sanborn figured out my real identity, but we have to make sure."

"And then?"

"There are a lot of suspects in terms of who killed Matthew."

"Can I help you narrow them down?"

"You sure you want to?"

Wilder puffed out his chest and flexed the muscles of one arm. "Haven't you heard? I'm MI6 now."

19

Wilder

"I usually have a lot more sophisticated equipment at my disposal," Wren said the next morning at breakfast.

Much like the night before, we got very little sleep as we wrung pleasure from each other. It felt different to me, though. Closer. More of the connection Wren had talked about.

"Should we ask Z to come in?" she asked.

"Do you usually work with him?"

"Not really."

"Why not?" I asked, smirking.

"He's MI5, Wilder," she answered, rolling her eyes.

"Bugger me, I can't even say anything!"

"About what?"

I told her about the conversation I'd had with George and how she'd condescendingly told me she didn't have any trouble with Wren because she was DHS. "I bet you could kick her ass, though."

Wren leveled her gaze at me. "I could kill her quicker."

I put my hands on my chest. "My God, woman, that was hot."

"Are you sure about this, Wilder? I mean, once the scent leaves the rose, will it still be as sweet?"

"Now that was flowery."

"You know what I mean."

"Are you afraid I won't think you're cool anymore?" I tried to sound like a California surfer, but it fell as flat as my attempt at a Southern accent the first day I met her.

"I'm serious."

"Then I will be too." I folded my arms on the table. "Last night, while you were snoring, I gave this a lot of thought."

"You said you'd be serious."

"I am. And you *were* snoring. But back to my point. Here's what I know about you, Kennedy King. You have a photographic memory. You carry more information in your brain than most people could learn in ten lifetimes. My guess is the real reason you were in the UK was to attend a meeting of the ASG, but it was thwarted by Caird's murder. The way you gather as much intelligence as you do is because no one on earth, except for me and I don't know who else other than Vera and your father, know who the hell you are."

I got up and poured her more coffee and then got myself another cup of tea.

"I know that anyone who sails a ship, flies an aircraft, makes national policy decisions, fights wars, locates targets, responds to natural disasters, or even navigates with a cell phone, relies on the NGA. And before you make fun of me for it, yes, I know that comes directly from the website."

"And you say I have a photographic memory."

"I can assure you, I don't. It took me several attempts to remember all of that."

"Last night?"

I raised a brow. "I did go through training, Miss King. I'll admit I don't know exactly what you do, but I don't care, because I know that ultimately, you're responsible for making sure the bad guys get what they deserve."

"Not directly, necessarily."

"Don't even think about selling yourself short."

"I have to tell you something else."

I'd been pacing, but sat down beside her. When she turned and looked directly at me, a pain had settled in the middle of my chest, and I needed an answer. "Last night you said there'd be no more lies."

"This isn't, or wasn't, a lie. And it isn't a secret. It's just something I've thought about."

"Out with it."

"For a while now, I've thought you would be an excellent addition to the NCGI."

"You're joking."

"I wouldn't joke about something like that."

She looked hurt, and that hadn't been my intention.

"What I meant is that I don't think I'm qualified."

"That's what training is for. What can't be taught, you already know. It's in your character, Wilder."

"I'm flattered."

"I'll admit you were on the right track at the hospital. Most of the work I do is with the NSA."

"NGA is yet another cover."

"So to speak. I mean, it's whom I work for. Just not in the capacity most people immediately think of."

"Sanborn was NSA."

"Yes. Before my time there, though."

"How long has it been?" I started doing the math. "Never mind. I'm feeling ancient."

"Wilder, don't fish. You're the handsomest man I've ever laid eyes on, and you well know it."

I was about to say something juvenile, but Kennedy fucking King was sitting beside me, so I refrained.

"There's a lot done at NCGI that isn't necessarily intelligence related," she said.

"And what fun would that be?"

"I agree."

"Can I ask you something else?"

"At this point, I'm an open book, Wilder."

"Z. Texas?"

"The ranch was handed down from my mother's family. He tried to make it work after she died, but his heart wasn't in it anymore. He eventually hired one of the ranch hands to manage the day-to-day operations—until Quint was old enough to take over."

"You said before that you and Quint don't talk much."

"It isn't as dramatic as I made it sound. We don't have much in common. I mean, I can get out and mend fences and even inseminate cows, but my heart isn't in it any more than Z's was. Quint loves it, though. He got more of our mama's blood."

"How old were you when your mother died?"

"Six."

I knew that the hard period at the end of the word meant she didn't want to discuss it, but like she said, we weren't going anywhere, and who knew when I'd have this chance again. "Tell me about her."

Wren looked into my eyes. I read what she was trying to convey loud and clear, but I chose to ignore it. "Tell me," I said again.

"She was beautiful," she said in a voice barely above a whisper.

"That isn't a surprise."

"I don't look anything like her."

"What do you remember about her?"

"She was a rodeo queen, and *fine*. Like spun sugar. I remember her hands were so delicate. She had long nails that she kept perfectly manicured. Even when she'd ride out on the ranch, she never broke a nail. I don't know why I remember that. Maybe because I bite mine."

I grasped her hand and kissed her fingertips.

"She had white-blonde hair. Quint got that. I don't know where I got mine. Z's hair is dark brown."

"Maybe from one of your grandmothers."

"That's where Finley Harlow came from, by the way. Finley was Z's mama's maiden name, and Harlow was my mama's mama."

Like when she told the story about the cow and the lightning, her accent went deeper with this one.

"She was smart. College educated. She and Z met at Oxford."

"He was a lucky man."

Wren stopped talking and looked into my eyes. "She didn't tell him her real name either."

I smiled. "Why not?"

"King?"

"I'm not following."

"King Ranch? It's the biggest ranch in all of Texas. Almost a million acres. My mama wasn't part of that King family, but whenever anyone heard the name, that's what they assumed. Z wouldn't have known the difference."

"What else, Wren?"

"She was affectionate. Always holding me when I went to sleep. She'd sing to me. I missed her so much when she was gone."

"Who took care of you then?"

"I did."

Two words and I knew the most important thing there was to know about Kennedy "Wren" King. She grew up the day she lost her mother, and she'd been fending for herself ever since. I didn't doubt that Z was a decent enough father, but I'd seen Z and Wren together. How could a father hide his love for his daughter as well as he did?

"I know what you're thinking."

"I'm thinking about Z."

"I do what I do today because of my father. Never once did he try to hold me back. I told you about the day Vera came to my graduation. Afterwards, I was so nervous about calling her. Z's exact words were, 'remember who you are and that she came to you.' It was all I needed to hear."

"I'm starting to like him a little more."

"He's your boss. You better like him."

"He's as much my boss as Sanborn is yours."

She laughed. "It isn't the same thing at all."

"You're right. Let's talk about Caird. You said there were many suspects, but are there? If he somehow got mixed up with United Russia, doesn't the list end there?"

"Not necessarily. It could be someone proving their loyalty."

"You have someone in mind."

"The most obvious are the fellow CSTO countries: Armenia, Belarus, Kazakhstan, Kyrgyzstan, and Tajikistan. None have the might of Russia, and one might need something UR is unwilling to give."

"What about Abkhazia and South Ossetia? Maybe they're hankering to be taken more seriously."

Wren smiled.

"You don't agree. What is it, five UN Security Council Members recognize them as sovereign nations, and one is Russia?"

"I'm smiling because of your earlier modesty. You're so much better than you know."

"I'm already prepared to lie at your feet and answer your every whim. You hardly need to flatter."

She rolled her eyes, and then in a blink of the same, she was back in work mode.

"China doesn't need a damn thing from Russia, nor does India."

"'Tis the other way around. At least when it comes to China."

"Russia needs the trilateral alliance to be more two-sided." Wren's eyes were hooded, and her expression grew dark.

"What are you thinking?"

"The reason the emergency NGA meeting was called was due to a recent negotiation between Russia and Turkey that took place in Moscow."

"I haven't heard a word about it."

"No one has."

"You have."

"Turkey is acquiring Russia's air defense system."

"And we have a winner, ladies and gentlemen."

Wren pulled out her phone and tapped the screen. Seconds later, I heard the front door open. I nodded when Z walked into the room where we were having breakfast.

"Would you like to join us, Pops?"

"She calls me Z," he snarled before his face broke into a proud smile that made me like the man a whole lot more. "You rang?" he said, walking over to Wren and leaning down to kiss her forehead.

"I need to get a message to Vera. Urgently."

Z nodded, pulled another phone out of the inside of his jacket, and handed it to her.

"Partiya Karkeren Kurdistan," she said followed by a pause. "Mormeht Savat." There was another pause. "Yes, I'm certain." She handed the phone back to Z.

"Certain?" I asked.

"Yes."

In the last twenty-four hours, I'd seen a myriad of emotions play out on Wren's face. This was new. Her steely, focused expression was as unnerving as the train of thought I hadn't been able to follow.

"What does the PKK have to do with Turkey acquiring Russia's air defense system?" I asked.

"It was a warning shot."

"I'm not following."

"Few can," murmured Z.

"Acquiring Russia's S-400 gives Turkey the ability to combat the PKK in a way they haven't had since the terrorist organization's founding in the mid-seventies. Savat is responsible for their 'special forces.'"

"What if you're wrong?"

"I'm not."

Z left, and Wren was quiet for the rest of the morning. Any attempt I made to coax her out of it was met with a sad smile that told me she wasn't ready.

"Let's take a walk around the grounds," I said when I reached the point where I felt powerless yet still compelled to do something.

"I'd rather not."

"You've spent the last three hours staring outside."

"Wilder, it's…"

I walked over and put my hands on her shoulders. "Tell me, Wren."

She shook her head, but I refused to relent. "Tell me," I repeated.

She shoved my hands away. "Do you not understand that I issued a death warrant this morning?"

"You said you were certain."

"I was. I am. It doesn't change the cold, hard truth that a man will die today and I'm the one who called it in."

"Are you having second thoughts?"

"Never."

I heard the front door open and, this time, anticipated Z's arrival.

"Mormeht Savat was killed in a counter-terror operation carried out in northern Iraq by Turkish forces."

Wren nodded and turned her back on both her father and me. "Any other casualties?" she asked.

"None, but I'll remind you, Savat and the PKK are responsible for the deaths of some twelve-hundred security personnel and civilians."

"Plus one," she murmured.

When Z left, I walked over and put my hands on Wren's shoulders. This time when she tried to shrug them off, I held tighter.

"Come with me." I took her hand and led her out of the room we'd spent far too much of the day in.

She didn't say a word as I led her upstairs and into the bedroom that had become ours.

I grasped the bottom of her jumper. "Arms up," I said, pulling it over her head. Once out of its confines, Wren dropped her hands to her sides.

Next I unfastened her trousers and pulled them over her bottom and down her legs along with her panties. I told her to step out, and she did.

Finally, I unfastened her bra, tossed it to the side, and led her over to the bed. I hated her resigned complacency, but that was why we were here. I had to break through the wall she'd erected since she made her call.

I brushed her hair away from her eyes, put my hands on either side of her face, and kissed her. As though the kiss had been a wrecking ball shattering her thin facade, Wren came alive in my arms. When she kissed me back, it was frenzied. She tugged at my clothes, making a sound that was a cross between a whine and a mewl.

"Slow down, sweetheart," I said, pulling my shirt over my head. Before I'd tossed it away, her hands were on my belt. I grabbed her wrists.

"Get on the bed," I demanded.

She let her hands go limp and padded over.

I was as naked as she was when I took her ankles and spread her legs.

She reached for me, but I took both of her hands and held them in one of mine. "My way, Wren."

I released her wrists, and she rested her hands near her sides.

She wanted it fast and hard, but I was going to give her the opposite. Starting on the soft skin inside her knee, I licked my way up her body and back down. Her back arched, and she writhed against me, but she didn't lift her arms. The only time she spoke was when she uttered the faintest "please."

"Put your arms around my neck," I said, resting my body on hers. "Wrap your legs around me." When she did, I slowly entered her wetness.

The orgasm I coaxed from her was long, slow, and deep. I waited until I felt her coming down from it before I let myself go.

Only then did Wren cry. I held her as sobs racked her body, scattering soft kisses on her forehead, cheeks, and eyelids.

When she finally stopped, she slept in my arms.

The question I'd asked earlier looped in my head along with her response.

Who took care of you then?

I did.

Not anymore.

20

Wren

It was mostly dark when I opened my eyes, but I knew it was morning. I eased out from under Wilder's protective hold and walked over to the window. Clouds shrouded most of the sun's light, but it still managed to cast a pinkish-orange glow on the grounds of the estate.

Yesterday, I'd refused Wilder's attempts to get me to tour the grounds. Today, I was anxious to.

My reaction once I'd made the call was part of a pattern I'd learned not to bother railing against. The only difference this time was that I didn't work my way through it alone. The tears would've come on their own, but not as quickly as Wilder had coaxed them out of me.

I looked over at his sleeping form. Soon we'd get the all-clear, and I'd be able to return to the States while Wilder went back to SIS and his new job with MI6. It was unlikely I'd be able to invent an excuse to come to England in the near future and, even then, a reason for us to work together.

When I saw Z walking across the yard toward the main house, adrenaline pulsed through my veins. Something must be seriously wrong for him to be coming to the house now. Had I sensed it? Is that why I'd inexplicably woken and walked over to the window?

I quickly put on my clothes, grabbed my boots, and closed the door behind me. I crept downstairs where I met my father, standing just inside the front door.

"What's happened?"

"There's been an escalation. The PKK has claimed responsibility for an attack on the US Embassy and Consulates in Ankara."

"Casualties?"

"Six dead, another thirty-five injured."

"There was no retaliation against Turkish forces."

Z shook his head.

"You need to make arrangements for me to leave, Z. Now."

When he didn't argue or even question my request, I knew that was why he'd come to the house in the first place.

Without a backwards glance, I followed him out of Wilder's uncle's house and to the vehicle waiting to transport me to the plane that would carry me back to the United States.

21

Wilder

I let the drapery fall, walked over, and put on my trousers. There was no point in rushing after Wren. By the time I got downstairs, she and Z would be gone, along with several other MI5 agents. I wondered how many would be left behind under the auspice of keeping me safe.

I'd wait another fifteen minutes and then be on my own way. My first stop would be at SIS headquarters. After that, I didn't know where I'd go.

Part 2

22

Wren

I'd forgotten how much I hated Texas in August when the average temperature hovered just above one hundred. I took off my hat and wiped the sweat from my brow with my shirtsleeve.

"Take a break," my brother shouted when I walked over to the truck to get some water.

I waved and nodded, but he rode up next to me anyway.

"Head back to the house."

"I'm fine, Quint."

"We're done for the day."

I pulled out my phone and checked the time. It wasn't even three o'clock. I took another long drink of water and walked back over to my horse. From where I stood, I could see the ranch house in the distance and the cloud of dust that swirled around the truck barreling up the gravel road that led to it.

"Who's that?" I asked.

"Somebody to see you."

I shielded my eyes from the sun and looked up at him. "Who?"

"She said her name was Darrow Whittaker and that she's a friend of yours from England."

The glare I shot him was pointless. Yeah, I was pissed he hadn't told me, but there was no way in hell Darrow would be driving onto our property if she wasn't being escorted by someone employed by the US government.

While I anticipated this day would come, Darrow wasn't the Whittaker I'd expected to show up unannounced.

"What's she want?" I said out loud without meaning to.

"What do friends usually want?"

My brother rode off in one direction while I turned my horse toward the trail that would lead me to where Wilder's sister waited.

As I got closer, I saw my father get out of the truck, walk around, and open the passenger door. By the time he came back around with Darrow, I was only a few feet from them.

"Z," I said, riding up and dismounting. "This is a surprise. Darrow, how are you?"

"Better now," she answered, running over to me. When I dropped Booker's reins, Z grabbed them.

"I'll take care of him," he said, walking away with my horse while Darrow and I embraced.

"What are you doing here?"

I saw the lines of hurt on my friend's face, but I couldn't do anything about that. Darrow had no more business showing up here than Z had bringing her.

"Axel and I broke up," she blurted. "That isn't the only reason I'm here, though."

"Come with me." I motioned for Darrow to follow me over to the porch.

"Should I get my bags?"

"Bags?" I immediately regretted the way it sounded. "We'll let Z get them," I added.

"I knew this was a bad idea," she mumbled.

"Whose idea was it?"

"Mine."

"How long are you visiting?" My voice sounded like my mother's when an unexpected guest arrived. Funny I'd remember something like that.

"You hate that I'm here."

I put my arm through Darrow's and patted her hand in the same way she'd done to me in England, only I was the one being comforted then. "I love that you're here. It's just a surprise."

Darrow fanned herself after we both sat down. "It's really hot here."

I laughed. "Understatement. Did you bring anything cooler you can change into?"

"Um…"

I laughed again. "It's okay. You can borrow some of my things."

"Thank you," Darrow murmured.

Did I dare ask? I closed my eyes and rested my head against the back of the rocking chair. "What happened between you and Axel?"

Darrow shrugged. "When…all that…happened after Matthew died, we went away, as I'm sure you know."

Actually, I didn't. I had no idea what had happened to anyone in Wilder's family, other than that they were safe, because I wouldn't allow anyone to tell me. My former assistant had been threatened within an inch of her life not to talk about the Whittakers, and until today, I hadn't heard a peep about them.

"Go on," I urged, wondering if I knew what I was getting myself into by encouraging her.

"Spending that much time together…we're really quite different."

"Sometimes that can be a good thing."

"Maybe for you—" Darrow stopped herself. "I mean, no. We weren't compatible." She shook her head. "Enough about that. It's really beautiful here."

As much as I'd been thinking about how I hated the heat of Texas a few minutes ago, I was thankful I'd been able to find sanctuary here after I left England. If there was any one person I could count on not to feel sorry for me or say a single word about Wilder Whittaker, it was my brother, Quint. Not that the name would've meant anything to him.

"I had a hard time picturing Z here, but he seems right at home."

I saw him come out of the barn with one of the Paints. He threw his leg over and went out in search of the crew. "You're aware he's my father?"

"Yes," Darrow answered. "He also told me that your real name is Kennedy Alexander, but that everyone has always called you Wren."

"I supposed he had no choice but to tell you the truth."

"Are you angry with him?"

"No," I answered, watching Z ride up to where Quint was working.

"I had to agree not to tell anyone as a condition of him bringing me here."

I shrugged. Did it really matter? It was inevitable that my Finley Harlow cover would soon be blown, if it wasn't already.

"Wren? About Sutton—"

"It isn't a topic open for discussion, now or ever," I snapped. "I'm sorry," I immediately added. "There are just…certain things."

"I understand. Stiff upper lip and all that."

I laughed out loud. "I really am glad you're here."

"It's a bloody good thing you are, or I'd be in quite a fix."

"Why do you say it like that?"

"Because I don't have any intention of ever going back to England."

By the time we finished dinner, Darrow appeared dead on her feet. After all, it was two in the morning in England. I showed her to the room in the wing where I'd asked Quint to put the bags, and then came back to the main part of the house, ready to get some answers.

Neither my brother nor my father was anywhere to be found.

I went out to the porch where Darrow and I sat earlier, leaned back in the rocking chair, and closed my eyes. It was cooler now but no less humid.

I hadn't realized until tonight how much Darrow looked like her brother—particularly her eyes, but her smile too. It didn't make me miss him more or the hurt inside me to worsen; that wouldn't have been possible. The only thing it did was make my longing more pronounced.

The porch boards creaked, but I didn't bother opening my eyes. "You are in so much trouble," I said to my father when I felt him sit down next to me.

"I couldn't say no."

"Why not? Did the Queen herself ask you to deliver Darrow to the colonies?"

"The woman was very convincing."

"Evidently, given you also took it upon yourself to tell her that you're my father, among other things you had no business divulging."

"It's been seven months."

I opened my eyes and looked over at him. "What do you mean?"

"The PKK has been all but annihilated, and the US government has threatened United Russia with sanctions that would cripple their economy if they didn't fall in line."

I got up to go into the house, but before I could open the door, Z grabbed my wrist. "Wren, it's time to let go."

"Of?"

"Whatever is stopping you from contacting Wilder."

"*That* is none of your business." I wrenched my arm away and went inside. On my way past the kitchen, I grabbed a rocks glass and a bottle of my favorite bourbon.

Instead of getting in bed when I knew I'd never sleep, I went back outside, this time on the private patio off my bedroom.

Seven months. Sometimes it felt more like seven days and others seven years, since I left the life I never dreamed I'd quit.

***

"Kennedy, this is a surprise," the woman most knew as Vera said when I stalked past her assistant and straight into the office.

"I'm resigning," I blurted.

"Take a seat."

"I have nothing more to say."

"Take a seat anyway," Amelia Watkins said without looking away from her computer screen.

I waited several minutes, tempted every few seconds to get up, walk out, and clean out my office, but I didn't. I owed Amelia more, but would concede at least that much.

Finally, my boss turned her chair, folded her hands on her desk, and looked straight at me. "While I said it was a surprise to see you, your resignation isn't. I've seen this coming for quite some time."

"You have?"

Amelia nodded but didn't say anything else.

I stood. "Thank you for everything you've done for me—"

"Sit back down. Here's what you're going to do instead of resigning."

***

I was nearly halfway through the year-long sabbatical Vera had insisted I take before making my final decision. She hadn't given me any choice about the time off, but at the end of it, I'd have many.

I could make my resignation official and live out the rest of my life as a private citizen. I could also come back to the exact job I'd had before. My other options were to work for another department at NGA, and finally, I could ask to be moved to another intelligence branch.

Most days, I knew I'd never go back to government work. Others, when I was bored out of my mind from endlessly counting cattle and doing the other mundane chores I saw as punishment but Quint insisted were simply part of running a ranch, I couldn't wait to get back to Washington.

As Vera had counseled me, my most important consideration was anonymity. If I walked away now, I could keep it. If I stayed with the NGA, it was unlikely I'd be able to.

The necessary precautions had been taken while I was in the UK, and while the PKK had found and killed Matthew Caird, my cover hadn't been blown.

As Z predicted, Amanda Sanborn's only real interest had been in Wilder Whittaker. I assumed the woman had been fired, but like everything else that had anything to do with Wilder, I refused to listen when the subject was broached.

All in all, I'd walked away relatively unscathed from an ordeal I'd never recover from.

If my life were a movie, I would've heard Wilder's name in the wind that defined what West Texans called their fifth season. Along with winter, spring, summer, and fall, there was wind.

It was rare for me to go many hours without finding myself daydreaming about the now MI6 agent. In that way, work would have been good for me. I'd have too much on my mind for it to drift.

Had I loved him? Did I still? The notion of it was too preposterous. We'd spent less than a week together, but those were days I'd remember for the rest of my life.

There were a few cowboys who poked around after hearing I was back in town, but like before, it was rare for me to go on a second date. It was ironic how I'd once thought the "soft-handed" Wilder could never measure up to the men I'd once considered rugged. No one I'd dated in the last few months came close to his brand of confidence, not that there had been many.

So often, when I was having a hard time making a decision about something, it would be his voice in my head that I'd listen to. It was as ridiculous as the idea that I'd loved him, but it got me through what seemed like endless days without him.

23

Wilder

I'd heard there was an SIS pool as to who would emerge bastard of the day—Pinch or me. I didn't care. There was work to be done, and anyone not interested in seeing to it, could bloody well sod off.

Rivet had finally been able to retire, and much to everyone's chagrin, mine included, he and the duchess had gone public with their wildly scandalous love affair.

There hadn't been a story like theirs since King Edward VIII unexpectedly abdicated the throne to marry Wallis Simpson.

The saddest part was that my father's name had been dragged through the proverbial mud when the scandal brought his past affair with Anna Caird to light as well as that he'd been Matthew's biological father.

Still, somehow, Rivet and Victoria had made it through, holding their heads high and never refraining from letting it be known they were in love.

Shiver had risen heroic from the same scandal's ashes when word of his valiant efforts to help his Russian-orphan wife and son escape the clutches of United Russia and bring her home to be Duchess of Bedfordshire had gotten out. Word was he was the peoples' first choice for knighthood.

While I hadn't officially been named head of MI6, I was acting chief, which everyone knew was merely a technicality until the Caird debacle faded in memory and I could be appointed without fanfare.

My second-in-command, Nate Thomason, was a world-class wanker, but if I'd also had three agents whom I outranked be offered the position of chief while I was continually looked over, I probably would've been an even bigger bastard than Nate was.

Rather than staying at the Kensington flat, when one became available in Sky Gardens, I immediately made arrangements to purchase the three-bedroom unit even though it was far more room than I needed for the limited amount of time I spent there.

The friendship between Pinch and me had survived our individual heartbreaks by us agreeing early on never to mention either woman involved in one another's presence. Although, Pinch did concede that he'd eventually have to let go of that, considering Darrow was my sister.

Neither spent time at Whittaker Abbey unless there was an urgent matter one or both of us had to attend to. Wellie had been ill in the early part of August, which meant we all took turns looking in on him. Shiver, Orina, and Darrow had checked in during the week, while Pinch and I filled in on the weekends. That was until Darrow left on a mysterious holiday, with no known end date, that everyone refused to talk about.

I avoided the drama until the gossip about it reached such annoying levels that I asked my brother where she was.

When Shiver summoned me to his office at the abbey to tell me that Darrow was in America, I left the room before my brother could say another word.

With August's summer bank holiday almost upon us, signifying the end of the season, I was trying to figure out a way to beg off attending the annual party the duchess had talked Orina and Shiver into throwing.

It seemed as though the evildoers in the world were also on holiday, given there wasn't a mission to be had in any direction I looked.

When my mobile rang and I saw it was Shiver calling, I considered not answering, but with Wellie's precarious health, I couldn't risk it.

"Hello, Shiv."

"You know what this call pertains to."

"I've been willing an international intelligence emergency, but so far none has materialized."

"For God's sake, Wild, is coming home really that bad?"

I didn't answer. I couldn't. It wasn't that bad; it was worse. Everywhere I looked, I saw Wren. Even in places she'd never been. And the others—where she had visited—threatened to bring me to his knees. I'd never imagined that such a profound sense of loss existed. The pain I felt whenever I thought of her, which was several times a day, cut me straight through to my core.

My sexual abstinence before I met Wren looked like a whim compared to my now-nonexistent desire to be with any other woman.

"Wilder? I'd ask if the call dropped, but I can hear you breathing."

"I'll be out sometime tomorrow or Sunday."

Shiver sighed. "Do better than that. I need your help. Lilliya has started teething, and Losha is at her wit's end."

At the same time my brother begged my assistance, Pinch walked in and sat down in my office.

"Of course. We'll be there."

"We'll?"

"Fulton and I will drive out together this afternoon," I said before ending the call.

"What the bloody hell did you just volunteer me for?"

"Summer Bank Holiday party at the abbey. Losha's got her hands full with the new baby."

"New? How old is she?"

"Three months."

"Is that still new?"

"Goodness," I said under my breath. "Yes."

"Bugger me," Pinch said, also under his breath. "Is it terrible that I literally hate being there?"

"I feel the same, mate."

"But you didn't—"

"Don't say it, Pinch." I stood and brushed everything on my desk into an open drawer. There'd be hell to pay from Mrs. Udele, who had volunteered to move offices with me, but that was the least amount of damage I could do without really making an ass of myself. "Let's get out of here."

I saw Thomason at his desk, but since his head was down, I didn't bother saying anything to the man. I certainly didn't need to check in with him when I left for the weekend, although Nate often alluded I should.

"What?" asked Pinch while we waited for the lift.

"Thomason. Can't stand the man."

"You aren't alone in that," Pinch said with hooded eyes.

I would ask if it was something personal, but given Thomason was with Section 6 and Pinch with MI5, it didn't make sense that it would be.

Pinch followed me down the block to Sky Gardens.

"I need to grab a bag from the flat," I told him.

"I'll come up."

"I'll just be a minute."

"God, mate, are you ever here?"

I came out bag in hand. "Not often, why?"

Pinch was standing with the door of my empty refrigerator open. "What do you eat?"

"What do you mean? You and I eat at the pub nearly every bloody night."

"What about breakfast?"

I shot him a look and walked out the door.

"You really don't eat any breakfast?" Pinch said when we got back on the lift.

"Not a big deal, Pinch."

"It's the most important meal of the day…"

I tuned him out, which was becoming a more frequent occurrence. Right now, the only thing I dreaded more than spending the weekend at Whittaker Abbey was the incessant talking I'd have to endure on the ride there.

"Why are you stopping here?" Pinch asked when I pulled up in front of Covington House.

"Sorry," I murmured, putting the Mercedes back in gear.

"By the way, what happened to the Jag?"

"Shop."

"Been in the shop going on a year now."

"It hasn't been that long." The truth was, it hadn't been in the shop at all. I just never drove it because, like so many other things, it reminded me of Wren.

I could see Pinch from the corner of my eye. "Been about seven months I reckon."

"You're walking on thin ice."

"I'm not the one who stopped at Covington House."

"We're a pair," I muttered as I continued on to Wellie's cottage.

"I fucking miss her," I heard my friend mumble.

I nodded. "I know."

24

Wren

By mid-September, the days rarely got warmer than ninety and it could drop as far as sixty-five at night. The first couple of weeks at the ranch were as hard on Darrow as my first weeks back had been.

She was a trooper and never complained, even when I would catch her tending blisters on her hands and feet at the end of a long day.

"I can do this," she'd say, as though Quint or I was going to kick her off the ranch if she didn't pull her weight.

Since our land was equal distance from Austin and San Antonio, we'd gone to each a few times so Darrow could pick up work clothes of her own. We'd even visited a couple of bars. While there was never a shortage of cowboys asking us to dance, like with dates, neither went for a second with the same guy.

I'd heard Darrow crying in her room after we'd said good night a few times. I'd done my own share of it, but it had to be so much worse for my friend. She'd known Axel all of her life; I'd only been with Wilder a handful of days.

I was clearing dinner dishes off the table when Darrow got up to help. "I'll get it. You can relax tonight," I said, pushing her back into the chair.

During the week, Quint, Darrow, and I often ate with the rest of the crew, but on the weekends, we usually went for a simpler dinner at the house. While we had a full-time cook who prepared most of our meals, I let her go early on Saturday and never let her work on Sunday, except during calving or branding season.

"There's a team-roping qualifier up in Belton tomorrow you might be interested in seein'," I heard Quint say to Darrow.

"That sounds like fun. Wren, do you want to go?"

I looked up from where I was scraping dishes and met my brother's eyes. "I'd love to, sweetie, but I have that report I have to finish up."

Report? Quint mouthed, making sure Darrow didn't turn around and catch him.

"Oh, well…"

"You should go," I pushed. "It's a lot of fun, and Quint and his partner are ranked pretty high this year."

"Okay. If you're sure."

"Positive," I said, smiling when my brother mouthed thanks, again behind Darrow's back.

It was quiet the next day with most everyone up at the rodeo, but I didn't mind. I slept in since Quint promised they'd get the morning chores done before they left, and at least part of the crew would be back in time to handle what needed to be done in the evening.

I pulled my French press out of the back of the cupboard and brushed the dust off. I got the bag of French roast out of the freezer where I kept it hidden behind the ice maker, and made myself a pot to savor. It wasn't quite as good as what I'd had when I was with Wilder, but it was close enough.

With a plate of fruit and a cup of coffee, I went out on the porch and sat in a rocking chair. My mother and I used to sit in one together before bedtime. In the summer, we'd watch the sun go down.

Like most everything, thinking about my mother reminded me of Wilder.

The first week I was back in the States, I'd checked my voice and email hourly, expecting to hear something from him. By the second, I'd tried to stop myself being disappointed until the end of each day when there was no word.

By the time I left for the ranch, I'd given up hope, but every once in a while, like when I saw the truck barreling down the road, carrying Darrow, I allowed myself to close my eyes and say a prayer that it was him. Usually it was a vendor or some friend of Quint's. The closest I'd gotten was his sister.

In some ways, having Darrow around made it easier, even though we never talked about him or Axel. In other ways, she was a constant reminder of what I'd walked away from.

There had been times I thought about initiating contact myself, but in the back of my mind, I could hear my mother's voice telling me that if a man wanted me, he'd move heaven and earth to find me, and if he never did, I'd have my answer. There was so little I remembered about my mother; it was odd I recalled that.

I might be harder to find if Z wasn't still DG of MI5. I knew my father, and if Wilder had asked, he would've told him I was at that ranch, especially since I'd never specifically asked him not to.

I tried to read, but the book didn't hold my interest. I went inside to take a nap, but couldn't. If I went for a walk, I'd only find a chore to do, and that would annoy me.

After piddling around in the kitchen, I walked to the back of the house where my mother's library remained exactly the way it had been when she died.

Running my hands over the books the housekeeper kept dust-free even though there was rarely anyone who came into this room, I looked down at the shelves of leather-bound photo albums. Each one bore an engraved nameplate that read "Alexander Family" and the year.

It was sweet that my mother had never used King-Alexander after she'd married Z, even though everyone referred to our family that way.

I pulled out the volume I recognized as being from the year my parents were married and ran my hands over the photos as I turned the pages.

There was no question my mother and father worshiped each other. It was sad to think that Z had never remarried even though my mother had died at such a young age. I remembered thinking twenty-eight was ancient, but now I was the same age and not only had I never been married or had children, I'd never experienced a love like my parents shared.

Or had I? It was a question I asked myself often, even though there'd never be an answer.

I opened my eyes and tried to focus when I heard voices calling my name.

"Where is she?" I heard Darrow ask.

"In here," my brother answered, switching on the lights.

I covered my eyes.

"What are you doing in here?" he asked.

"I must've dozed off looking at pictures." Before I could pick up and close the photo album that had slipped off my lap, Darrow grabbed it.

"Oh my goodness," she gasped, setting the heavy leather book on a table. "That's my mother and father."

"Seriously?" said Quint, looking over Darrow's shoulder and making me feel as though I was intruding on a private moment.

"Look, Wren," she said, holding out her hand.

"I didn't realize Z knew the duke," I said, looking over Darrow's other shoulder.

"Of course he did. My father was the one who helped Z get the job with SIS," she said, pointing to the couple seated with Z standing behind them.

I covered my mouth in time to stifle my gasp. It was as though I was looking at a photo of Wilder.

25

Wilder

"I hate the bloody holidays," said Pinch, plopping down in my office chair like he did so often. "This isn't even one of ours."

"Haven't you read the news? One in three Brits now celebrates Thanksgiving."

"Why does your family have to be among them?"

"You can beg off."

"You know I can't. My father…"

Pinch didn't finish, and I didn't want him to. Any conversation we had about Wellie's declining health ended with both of us wondering why Darrow hadn't come home yet, even though neither of us said it out loud. Until today.

"She's like his bloody daughter," said Pinch, putting his head in his hands.

"I'll take care of it." I stood and squeezed his shoulder before leaving in search of Z.

"Whittaker," said Z when I walked in. "Surprised to see you here."

"Likewise," I answered, even though we had two entirely different reasons. "I need a favor."

Z had looked up, but with my request, he leaned back in his chair and steepled his hands. "What do you need?"

"I need to reach Darrow. Wellie's quite ill, and I fear if she doesn't come home now, she might regret not doing so."

"I see," he said, moving his steepled fingers closer to his mouth. "Have you asked her to come before now?"

"I'm quite certain Shiver would have done so."

The man raised a brow. "Okay. I'll assist."

"Thanks, Z," I said, turning to leave the office.

"Where are you going?"

"Heading to the abbey. Have a pleasant Thanksgiving," I said. "I suppose you do celebrate it, given you were married to an American."

Z held out a piece of paper.

"What's this?" I asked, walking back to the desk to take it from him.

"Where you can reach Darrow."

I hesitated, but before I could speak, Z did.

"I'll not do it for you, Whittaker. You want her home, call her yourself. If I hear you passed this off to Mrs. Udele, I'll never grant you another favor for as long as I live."

"Bugger me," I grumbled once I was far enough from Z's office that he wouldn't hear me. This was hardly something I could hand off to Pinch either.

I folded the paper and stuffed it in my pocket.

"Any luck?" Pinch asked when I walked back in.

"I had a chat with Z."

"Thanks, Wild," said Pinch. "You ready?"

"Just a few loose ends to tie up. I'll meet you at the pub."

Pinch waved behind him as he walked out.

After spending ten minutes staring at my desk phone, I picked it up and dialed the number scrawled on the paper. It rang several times, and just as I was about to hang up, I heard her voice.

"Thank you for calling King-Alexander Ranch. If you're trying to reach Quint, please call the office phone." I listened as Wren's sweet voice rattled off another number. "Otherwise, leave a message, and we'll call you back."

I took a deep breath and placed the phone back in its cradle. This wasn't the kind of message one left on voicemail. I'd try again once we reached the estate. In the meantime, I prayed that when I did, anyone but Wren would answer.

I'd taken to staying at the abbey, telling Shiver and Orina that if I did, I could spend more time with my niece and nephew. However, after two straight hours of endless crying by the unhappy Lilliya along with Kazmir's ruckus, I begged off to Dorchester House, saying I had phone calls to make and I'd be back later.

In truth, I only had one call to make, and I dreaded it. Seven here meant it was either eleven or noon in the States, or was it earlier? How early had it been when I called before?

I pulled out my mobile and checked the zone for Dallas. It was in the center of Texas; it should be the same time there as wherever Wren and Darrow were.

I breathed a sigh of relief when I saw there was only a six-hour difference, which meant it had been ten when I called earlier. A very respectable hour.

Pulling the crumpled paper out of my pocket, I punched the number into the phone.

For the second time, I got the recording. I listened through to the end anyway, just to hear Wren's voice.

I walked through the house I'd only been in a handful of times since I'd returned from Cumbria in January. Pouring a brandy, I went into the study, lit a fire, and sat in the same chair I had the night I'd tucked Wren into bed upstairs.

I fucking missed her, as Pinch so often mumbled about Darrow. Hearing her voice hadn't made it better or worse. The pain I felt was at a constant level of torturous.

I counted every hour that passed, until finally, at midnight, I decided to try once more tonight.

It rang twice.

"King-Alexander Ranch," the voice on the other end said.

"Hello, Wren? This is Wilder."

26

Wren

"Hello? Is anyone there?" I heard Wilder say.

"Um, yes. Sorry. Hello, Wilder."

"Wren."

The way he said my name, I wanted to reach through the phone and touch him. Not just touch him, kiss him, and so much more.

"How are you?" he asked.

"I'm okay. You?"

"I've had three of Wellie's brandies, so if you're really asking, I'm apt to tell you the truth."

"I'm asking."

I heard his sharp intake of breath, followed by a long release of the same, and then something else. Was that a fire crackling in the background?

"Where are you?"

"Dorchester House, which is odd because I never come here anymore."

"Why not?"

I heard more of the crackling fire and what sounded like him taking a sip.

"Wilder?"

"Because you're here. Everywhere I look."

My eyes filled with tears. I had to end this conversation before I began to sob. "Why did you call?"

"Right," he said, clearing his throat. "It's about Wellie."

"What's wrong?" I gasped.

"He isn't well."

"I'm sorry," I said a second time, wishing Darrow was home so I could hand the phone off to her, but she wasn't. She and Quint were out for dinner.

"I'm calling to ask Darrow if she could please come home. I fear if she doesn't, she won't make it in time."

Tears rolled down my cheeks.

"Are you there?"

I nodded, knowing he couldn't see, but I was unable to get the words out to answer.

"Wren, if you are still there, I want you to know… Bugger me—" I heard the phone rustling. "I want you to know…"

The call ended, but I clung to the phone's receiver anyway while tears slid down my cheeks. Soon I was doubled over, crying harder than I had in months.

That's the way Quint and Darrow found me when they came in only minutes later.

"Wren, what's happened?" asked Darrow, racing over to me with Quint on her heels.

"Is it Z?" he asked.

I shook my head. How could I explain to Darrow that I was crying this hard over a man I'd never met? I couldn't, because I wasn't. I was crying over Wilder.

"Please, Wren. Tell us," said my brother.

"It was Wilder," I said between sobs.

Darrow covered her mouth. "What's happened?"

"It's Wellie."

"Oh, God, no. Not Wellie." Darrow broke down and cried as hard as I was while my poor brother tried to comfort us both.

I managed to curb my tears first. "I'm so sorry to worry you this way, Darrow. He's ill, and Wilder has asked that you please come home as soon as possible."

Quint put his arm around Darrow's shoulders, and she rested her head on his chest. Feeling as though I was interrupting an intimate moment between them, I went to my bedroom, closed the door, and cried myself to sleep.

When I came out of the bedroom the next morning, puffy-eyed and hoping to avoid human contact, my brother was sitting at the kitchen table, waiting for me.

"I booked the tickets," he said when I walked over to pour a cup of coffee.

"Thank you for doing that, Quint. I'm sure Darrow appreciates your help and support very much."

"Your flight leaves in three hours."

"Her flight."

Quint stood. "No, your flight, Wren. Darrow is in no condition to fly to London alone, and you know I can't go with her; we're about to head into the thick of fall calving season."

"I can't go!" I gasped.

"Are you telling me you're going to stay here and handle the calves?"

I shook my head.

"I didn't think so. That means you're going because there isn't any way I'm going to let her go alone, and there's no one else."

I thought through what my brother was saying. I could do this. I'd get Darrow to London, have Z meet us at the airport and take her to Whittaker Abbey, while I caught the next flight back to the States.

"You're right. I'll do it."

The goodbye between Quint and Darrow was as awkward as I imagined Wilder found it when she was with Axel. It hadn't occurred to me earlier, but thank heavens my brother wasn't traveling with Darrow. It was Axel's father who was ill, and that would be incredibly unfair to him.

For the fourth time in the last three hours, I called every number I had for Z, leaving messages at each while trying to avoid Darrow overhearing.

"This is Wren again," I said. "I need you to meet us at Heathrow tomorrow morning. No, wait. It isn't tomorrow; it's the following morning. Disregard my other messages. Anyway, Z, I need you to meet us at eight…" What day was it? "Um, Friday morning. I beg you, Z. If that isn't right, figure it out. We're boarding now. Oh, and if you haven't gotten the other messages, I'm traveling with Darrow Whittaker, and she needs you to take her out to the abbey as quickly as possible."

"Who was that?" Darrow asked when I joined her at the gate. "Was that Wilder?"

"No, sweetheart. I was calling Z."

"Why?"

"He's going to meet us at the airport."

"Why?" she asked again.

I put my hand on the small of Darrow's back, navigating her toward the flight attendant who was asking for all first-class passengers to board.

"He's going to give us a lift to the abbey," I lied. It wasn't a big lie. He would be delivering Darrow.

"But Wilder's picking us up. I spoke to him just after Quint purchased the tickets."

"Okay, then. Wilder is picking us up," I agreed, pushing Darrow toward the plane and praying my plan would still work.

It was a prayer I said several times over the course of the next ten hours while Darrow slept. I wondered if she'd taken something. I wished I would have. It was too late now though; we'd be arriving in under two hours.

"Great news," the pilot said minutes later. "We'll be landing forty-five minutes early. That's seven forty-five London time."

Like me, most of the first-class cabin murmured sounds of appreciation. It was a lucky break, given it was unlikely Wilder would arrive at the earlier time, but Z definitely would. He was a stickler about flight times. He always had been. He'd check, and he'd be there to meet us, and Wilder wouldn't.

"Wake up, sweetie," I said to Darrow, rubbing her arm. "We're getting ready to land."

She sat straight up and looked at her watch. "Already? Did I really sleep the entire flight?"

"You did," I answered, envying her. It was okay, though. Soon I'd be on my way back to the States, and this time I'd be the one to take something that would put me to sleep.

As the pilot taxied the plane to the gate, I not only prayed, I crossed my fingers, and if I'd been able to in my boots, I would've crossed my toes too.

I got Darrow situated, off the plane, and almost through customs when I saw Axel waiting on the other side of the glass. I breathed a sigh of relief as much as sorrow that it was his face I saw rather than Wilder's, but it was what I'd wanted.

Now all I had to do was get Darrow to him, get over to the ticket counter, pick up my boarding pass for my return flight, and then get back through customs and security before it left. I checked her watch. Thanks to our early arrival, I had almost three hours. I should be on the other plane in plenty of time.

Given my credentials, both of us were through customs in record time. I stood back as Darrow ran into Axel's arms, thankful my brother wasn't here to see their reunion. I checked my watch again. It was probably too soon for me to turn and run, so to speak, but soon I'd let Darrow know my plans and be on my way.

"Excuse me," I heard a voice say from behind me.

I quickly apologized and took a step to the left, out of the man's way.

"Hello, Wren," said another man I bumped into and whose arms were grasping both of mine, holding me upright. "It's nice to see you."

"Wilder?"

27

Wilder

"Come with me," I said, taking Wren by the hand. I knew I sounded abrupt, but I had so much to say, and I didn't want to do it in front of an audience.

"Wait," she said, trying to free herself from my grasp.

By then we were far enough away from the crowd of people trying to get past customs that I stopped. I didn't let go of her hand, though. Instead, I turned and faced her, gazing into the most beautiful eyes I'd ever seen on the most beautiful face with the most beautiful smile. Although she wasn't smiling at the moment.

I cupped her face with my palm and wiped away the tear that ran down her cheek.

"Do you have any idea how much I've missed you?"

Wren's gaze met mine, but she didn't speak; she only shook her head. She looked away as more tears ran down her cheeks. I put my arm around her shoulders and pulled her close.

"I wish you'd talk to me."

"What is there to say?" she murmured.

I leaned back, cupping her cheek with my palm again. "There's so much."

"My flight…I need to go," she said, shaking her head.

"What do you mean?"

"I'm flying back to the States."

"But you just got here."

"I have no reason to stay."

I felt the air leave my lungs. Had I really meant so little to her? If that were the case, why had she confided so much in me?

"When is your flight?"

"Eleven."

I looked at my watch. I had a little over two hours to convince her not to leave, at least not so soon. I looked around; while we weren't in the midst of a throng of people any longer, where we were, certainly wasn't private.

"Let's please find somewhere we can talk."

"Wilder…"

"I'm begging, Wren."

She took several deep breaths while our eyes held. "Okay," she finally answered, her voice barely above a whisper.

There was a security office on the next concourse over. Perhaps I could finagle a way for us to talk there. With my arm still around her shoulders, I led her away from the customs area. I saw Pinch waiting with Darrow nearby and shook my head, hoping neither would approach. I didn't want to share Wren with anyone right now. I had so little time to make my case.

Thankfully, Pinch nodded, leading Darrow in the opposite direction.

When we reached the office, I knocked and then showed the officer who opened the door my credentials.

"Can I help you, sir?" the woman asked with wide eyes.

"May I make use of this room for a few minutes?"

"Of course," she said, scurrying past us. Thankfully there was no one else inside.

"Would you like to sit down?" I asked, closing the office door.

"I've been sitting for several hours."

"Understood."

Now that I had her alone, my mind raced with where to begin. "It's nice to see you."

"Thank you." She looked everywhere but at me.

"There are so many things I want to say to you, but I don't know where to begin," I confessed.

"Didn't you say it all when you called?"

I watched as her eyes filled with tears and she turned away. I got up and walked around her so I could see her face. I held her still when she tried to turn away a second time.

"I don't feel as though I had time to say anything."

"Why are you doing this?"

I sat on the edge of the desk behind me, put my hands on her waist, and pulled her close to me. "What is it you think I'm doing?"

"Why are you insisting we talk? When you called…"

We were going around in circles. I had no idea what she was referring to, and it didn't appear she was going to tell me.

"I may have had a brandy or two, but I remember our conversation, Wren. Of this much, I'm absolutely certain—the very last thing I said before you ended our call was that I miss you so much I can't breathe. Is that what has you so upset? If it is, I can't help it nor will I apologize for saying it. That's how I feel."

"You ended our call, and you didn't say you missed me."

"I don't want to argue with you. Please tell me what I can say or do that will allow us to move past this."

Wren folded her arms and raised her chin. "What about when you said you stay away from Whittaker Abbey because everywhere you looked you saw me?"

"Yes. What of it?"

She tried to wiggle out of my grasp, but I wouldn't relent.

"Yes, Wren, everywhere I look I see you. Even places you never were, because I imagine taking you there. And the places where we were…that's harder." I reached up with one hand and smoothed the wrinkle in her brow. "God, I wish you'd tell me what you're thinking."

"I thought you meant…"

I stood, still keeping one arm firmly around her. "You thought I meant stay away because I didn't want to be reminded of you? It's true, but not in the way you're thinking. It was too painful, Wren."

"But you didn't…"

"Didn't what?"

She shook her head, trying again to look away. As soon as I thought we were getting somewhere, she'd pull back, and it was making me angry. I'd just confessed how much I'd missed her, but she didn't say she felt the same.

"What didn't I do, Wren? Come after you?"

When she didn't respond, even with a nod of her head, I got angrier.

"If that's what you're asking, how in bloody hell could I have done that? Do you know that when I went down to the garage, Z had had my car disabled? What was I to do, *run* after you? You'd already warned me that if I did, I'd be shot." The more I talked, the louder my voice got. I knew it, and I didn't care. "Did you really think I'd come after you when you sneaked off before the sun came up without as much as a kiss goodbye?"

"I had no choice."

"Really? No choice. You couldn't have looked up at the window where I stood watching, and at least waved? Or better yet, you couldn't have woken me and asked me to come with you?"

"The PKK...they retaliated."

"Yes, I was made aware." I shook my head.

"I was keeping you safe."

"As. Was. I. You."

"Why didn't you...?"

"What? Finish the question. Why didn't I, what? Because I can assure you, whatever you're going to ask, I did."

"You didn't contact me."

"How would I have done that? It was as though you fell off the bloody earth."

"Z."

I laughed. "Z. Right. Ask your father how many times I begged him to tell you I was trying to reach you."

"Begged?"

"Begged."

"I didn't ask him not to."

"Evidently, he was trying to protect you too. From me. The man who loved you, for bloody sake."

"Loved?"

"No, Wren, not loved. Love." I waited, praying she would at least react. I'd just poured every bit of my heart onto the floor. If that wasn't enough for her, we were finished. I had no more to give.

Slowly she raised one hand to my cheek, and then with an equally frustrating languidness, she reached up and brought her lips to mine.

I couldn't hold back. I put my hand on the back of her neck and forced her mouth open with my tongue.

When her arms went around me, I deepened our kiss and pulled her body flush with mine.

The idea that she was about to get on a plane and leave again made me want to cry out in protest, but if that was what she wanted, how could I stop her?

"Wren?" I said, pulling away. "Stay. Please. Stay. I don't know what else I can say—"

She put two fingers on my lips. "Okay. I'll stay."

I looked up at the ceiling and then back at her. "You'll stay?"

She smiled and nodded. "Yes."

"Let's get out of here." I picked up the bag I didn't notice she'd dropped on the floor when we came into the security office.

"Do you have other luggage?"

"No."

I raised a brow.

"I wasn't staying."

"Where are we going?" Wren asked when I went east toward London rather than north.

"I have a flat at Sky Gardens. I thought we could use some time alone before going to the abbey."

She was here. She was staying for an indeterminate amount of time, but there was so much we needed to talk about. "Will that be all right?"

"Of course."

I covered her hand with mine, wishing I could magically transport us back to Cumberland, or before, at the abbey. I'd missed her so much, but I still wasn't with her. A part of her, the part I loved so much, was still closed off to me.

We'd had six whirlwind days and four nights, followed by months apart. Did she believe me when I said I loved her? Could she? Sometimes I couldn't believe it myself, but I knew what I felt.

"There's a daily pool at the office as to whether Pinch or I is the bigger wanker."

She smiled. "Who's typically the winner?"

"Me. I believe it's ten to one at this point."

"How's MI6?"

"Bloody boring as ever. I'm sure you heard I'm interim chief."

"I hadn't."

I looked over at her, somewhat surprised. "No?"

"I haven't kept up."

I wasn't sure what to say. How was it possible for her to do her job and not know who the chief of MI6 was?

"I'm not at the NGA anymore. At least not for now." She had her head against the back of the seat and was looking out the window.

"I see."

I pulled into the underground parking garage, suddenly feeling inexplicably anxious. "You're sure you're okay with this?"

"I'm sorry if I've given you the impression I'm not. I haven't slept or eaten in hours."

"Oh. That isn't good."

"I'll be okay once I get some food in my stomach."

"Right. That's the not-good part. I don't keep much here."

"Just some fruit would be fine."

"Yes, well…"

"Not even fruit?"

When I shook my head, she smiled. "Poor planning, Whittaker. Hard to woo the woman if you don't keep her nourished."

I climbed out of the Jaguar, the car I hadn't driven since the day after she left me in Cumbria, and walked around to open the passenger door. When I held out my hand and she took it, my nerves quieted.

So many times, I'd asked myself if I was making more of our brief time together than it was, but when I touched her, when she smiled, a sense of peace came over me. It was a feeling I hadn't known before Wren, and I'd missed it profoundly once it was gone.

"Wilder?"

I had no idea how long I'd been standing still, my hand cupping her face, staring into her eyes. "I missed you so."

She leaned into me. "Should we go up to your flat?"

"Right. So, food. Leadenhall is just around the corner. Should we—"

"Do they have delivery service?"

28

Wren

I stood near the window and took in the view of the Thames and SIS headquarters. I could hear Wilder's voice as he placed an order with the market, and I could feel the cold from outside when I put my hand near the window, and yet it was so surreal it was as though I wasn't actually here.

"Where have you gone?" Wilder asked, running his fingertip down my cheek. His touch was so familiar, yet so foreign.

"I can't believe I'm here."

"Having a hard time believing it myself."

"What are we doing, Wilder?"

"Come sit with me." He pulled me over to the sofa, flipping a switch on the wall to light the fireplace. "Not as impressive, but it is convenient."

I sat on the far end of the sofa; Wilder stood in front of it.

"This is bloody awkward," he mumbled, finally sitting in the center. He turned slightly so he was facing me, and our legs touched. "What did you mean when you said you aren't at the NGA anymore?"

"I tried to resign. Vera insisted on a leave of absence instead." I waited, but he didn't respond. "Please say something."

He shook his head, scrubbed his face with his hand, and stood. "Can I get you anything to drink? Because I'll tell you, I sure as hell need something."

I watched as he pulled out a familiar-looking bottle.

"How much of that stuff does Wellie make?"

Wilder pulled out the cork and poured two glasses. "My guess is, more than we can drink in a lifetime."

When he handed me one of the glasses, I set it on the table. He downed what was in his and poured another.

"I have imagined this so many times, and yet I never dreamed this is what it would be like," he said, pouring a third shot and then coming to sit next to me again.

"Uncomfortable?"

"It's so much worse than that. Am I wrong?"

"You're not."

"I don't know how to get past it."

Wilder's phone vibrated, and he got up. "That'll be the delivery."

When I went into the kitchen, I found two men delivering bags upon bags of groceries that Wilder was looking for places to put.

"What did you do, order the entire market?" I tried not to laugh, but the look on his face was more than I could overcome. Soon I was doubled over, hand resting on the counter, laughing so hard I was back to crying.

I put my hands over my face to stop, but it was too late; my giggles were uncontrollable. I looked over, and Wilder was laughing too, trying to sign for the delivery, tip the men, and usher them out.

When he came back into the kitchen, I was still giggling.

"They think we're crazy," I said.

"I did get a bit carried away."

I walked over to where he stood and put my arms around his waist. "You really are so sweet."

Wilder grasped the back of my neck and kissed me. He put his arm behind my knees, lifting me into his arms. With one hand, he grabbed a banana before carrying me into the bedroom, not taking his lips from mine until he set me on the bed.

I giggled again when he peeled the top of the banana and then presented it to me with a bow.

"Nourishment. And Wren?" He waited until my eyes were on him. "The only sounds on earth sweeter than hearing you giggle are the ones I am about to coax from your beautiful lips."

If anyone had told me a week ago that I'd be here with Wilder, not to mention in his bed, I would've thought they'd lost their mind. I wasn't sure mine was functioning quite right either.

"Let me see you, Wren." He pulled his shirt over his head and then waited for me to do the same. Next, I tugged off my boots and then slid the leggings I'd worn on the plane over my hips and down my legs.

"I like the purple," he said, fingering the lace on the bra that matched my panties. "I might want you to keep these on for a bit."

Wilder dropped his pants and came to lie beside me. "I told you that I'd only ask this once, but I find myself doing it a third time. Is this what you want, Wren?"

"More than anything," I answered, looking deep into his beautiful black-brown eyes. "I missed you so much, Wilder."

He closed his eyes and let out a deep breath. "I can't tell you how I've longed to hear you say those words."

I touched his face. "I felt so empty. I told myself it was leaving the NGA, but my heart knew it was because I wasn't with you."

Wilder brought my hand to his lips and kissed it. "Why did you stay away?"

Why had I? At first it was because I had to be certain the threat from the PKK was contained. Then, there had been United Russia to deal with. Neither of those were things I had to manage myself, but I couldn't allow myself to bring more danger to Wilder or his family. There was a part of me that still felt responsible for Matthew Caird's death—no matter how many times my father tried to convince me otherwise.

"At first it was about protecting you, and then, when I didn't hear from you…"

"You convinced yourself I didn't want you."

"I am, or was, very good at my job, Wilder. The rest of life, not so much."

"You sell yourself short. There are so many amazing things about you, my precious little bird, that have nothing to do with what you do for a living."

"You're sweet, but—"

Wilder growled, sunk his teeth into the soft part of my neck, and then kissed the nip away. "I am anything but sweet, woman."

29

"My kitchen is overrun with bags of food, some of which should really be in the refrigerator, and yet the only thing I hunger for is more of you." I nipped the flesh just above Wren's hip.

In the last two hours, I'd explored every inch of the body I'd yearned so hard to hold. Hearing her cries of pleasure, sinking deep inside of her—her mouth, her tongue, her fingers—as soon as I swore I could do no more, I'd be ready to begin all over again.

"Did you hear me, love?" I asked, running my fingers through her hair as she kissed her way down my body.

"I'm feeding my own hunger."

"I fear you're insatiable."

"You shouldn't have kept me waiting for nine months."

"Nine months? No. Sorry. It was longer than that."

"Okay, nine and a half."

I put my hand on the side of her face. "Look at me."

Wren scooted up and rested her chin near my heart.

"Three hundred and three days. Or, if you're fixated on months, it was nine months and twenty-nine days. As of your flight landing this morning, or rather when I finally saw your beautiful face as you walked out of customs, it had been seven thousand, two hundred, and seventy-two hours since I watched you walk out of my life, feeling powerless to stop you."

She put her arms around me and squeezed tight. "I had no idea you even thought about me."

"Did you think I could've forgotten you?"

"I didn't know," she whispered.

I could feel her tears on my bare skin. "There's something I don't know, Wren, and I need to." I lay on my side and pulled her up so her head was on the pillow next to mine. I brushed her hair away from her face and kissed both of her cheeks. "I need you to tell me how you feel. Even if it isn't what I want to hear, I need to know."

Wren took a deep breath and looked into my eyes. "You are the first—the only—man who has held my heart. I love you now, and I will love you until the day I die."

30

Wren

"I promise, by noon. No later," I heard Wilder say. "Yes, she's right here." He passed the phone to me.

"Hello, Darrow."

"I thought perhaps the two of you had been swallowed by a black hole. You missed Thanksgiving."

I laughed. "We flew through Thanksgiving, and you slept the entire time."

"Mrs. Mollybock made quite a feast followed by an equally dramatic fuss when her precious Sutton didn't arrive for dinner. You do know he's her favorite."

"Mrs. Mollybock?"

Wilder groaned.

"The cook. There's only two people she gives a wit about, Sutton and Wellie. The rest of us could eat porridge morning, noon, and night for all she cares."

"Speaking of Wellie, how is he doing?"

"Much better, thank God."

"I can't wait to meet him."

"I keep forgetting you haven't. You must hurry and get up here. Tell Sutton he's not allowed to hold you hostage any longer."

"I will. We're leaving soon, I promise. Oh, and I may need to borrow some clothes."

Darrow laughed. "Right, of course. Um, Wren, I have a question."

"Go ahead."

"Hang on one minute."

I scrunched my eyes and looked at Wilder, who shrugged.

"Okay, I've gone outside. Have you spoken to Quint?"

"I haven't. To be honest, I haven't spoken to anyone other than your brother."

"I was just wondering. We'll talk more when you get here."

"What was that about?" Wilder asked when I ended the call.

"Something I'd much rather have your sister tell you herself, but that may be even more awkward." I took a deep breath. "Darrow and my brother were…involved."

"Bugger me," muttered Wilder, sitting on the edge of the bed we'd hardly left. "What about Pinch?"

"You saw them as well as I did at the airport. She seemed very happy to see him."

"I didn't, actually. I mean I did, but I was so concerned about you, and I've grown so used to not paying attention to them." He ran his hand through his hair. "You do remember I told you about the office pool?"

I nodded.

"He was as miserable as me, and it was because of my sister."

"I kind of figured that."

"How serious are they? Were they?"

"I know my brother really cares about her, but serious? I have no idea."

"Flipping heck," he mumbled, shaking his head.

"I'm not sure there's anything I can do."

"No, no. I don't expect you to. There isn't anything I'd do either. My sister has certainly put her foot in it, though."

"Do you know what happened between her and Axel? Do you know why she left England and came to Texas?"

"No idea. In fact, I didn't know she'd left, and I certainly didn't know where she'd gone."

"Hmm."

"We're awfully clueless for two whizzes of the intelligence world," he said, pulling me over to sit on his lap.

"You're the whiz. I'm former."

"About that. Your leave of absence will soon expire."

"Not until February." I'd told Wilder the options Vera had given me and that I still wasn't sure I wanted to return to the NGA.

"I hate to bring this up, but whatever happened to Sanborn?"

I shuddered. "I don't know exactly. Vera said she'd handle it."

Wilder raised a brow.

"What?"

"I may have to do a little digging on that one. When you said you hadn't kept up, you really didn't."

"I don't know if I can go back to that life, Wilder."

"There is nothing that says you have to, my darling. You could always come to work for MI6."

"Very funny."

He kissed my cheek. "Nothing that has to be sorted now. Let's get on the road before Darrow sends a search party."

31

Wilder

"I'd love to see this place in spring and summer," Wren said when we drove through the gates of Whittaker Abbey.

I brought her hand to my lips. "And you shall."

While we hadn't talked about much beyond the day ahead, other than the decision Wren would have to make regarding her career, that didn't mean our future wasn't on my mind.

She'd not said anything about returning to the States, and I certainly wouldn't open that can of worms in front of my sister.

With my new position at MI6, it wouldn't be easy for me to take an extended holiday. On the other hand, as the last few months had proven, my life wasn't worth much if Wren wasn't in it.

"Where have you gone off to?" Wren asked, borrowing the phrase I so often used with her.

"I'm here." I smiled. "Very much here, in fact. Thinking about you and me."

"And?"

"That's all. Nothing else is of concern." I pulled up to the front of the abbey. "It looks as though we're not the only arrivals from London."

It appeared my mother, Rivet, and Z had pulled up shortly before we had. Pinch and Shiver were helping with their bags.

"Full up at the abbey tonight," I said, opening Wren's door.

"Good to see you, finally," said Shiver, setting the bags he was carrying down to greet Wren.

"Hello, Shiver," she said, kissing both of his cheeks.

"Losha and Darrow are inside, both anxious to see you."

"Not before her father," said Z, coming up to hug her.

"You are in so much trouble," I heard her mutter.

"A state I often find myself in, it seems," he laughed.

"Sutton, please introduce us," said the duchess, also coming over to meet Wren.

"Of course, Mother, but can we please go inside? It's starting to rain."

While everyone else hurried in, I hung back, Wren's hand firmly grasped in mine.

"It's hardly sprinkling," she said, smiling up at me.

"I know, but I needed to do this before you're whisked away from me."

I pulled Wren into my arms and kissed her. "I love you, my Wren."

"I love you, Wilder."

"Remember, we aren't staying a minute past dessert."

"Sutton?" shouted my mother from just inside the front door. "We're waiting."

"Before we go in, how shall I introduce you?"

She sighed. "I don't think it matters much at this point, at least within your family, given you and your brother, Rivet, and even Pinch either work or have worked for SIS."

"Shall we, then?"

"I may need another kiss first."

I smiled and indulged her, something I would gladly do as often as she liked.

"Wren, I'd like you to meet my mother, Duchess Victoria. Duchess, this is Kennedy King-Alexander, affectionately known to all as Wren."

I watched my mother carefully as she visibly assessed the woman I loved. While I respected her very much, she had a catty side I'd not tolerate when it came to Wren.

"It's lovely to meet you," said the duchess as the two shook hands.

"Likewise, ma'am."

"Is that Wren?" I heard my sister come in from the other room, and I cleared my throat.

"What?" She looked at me with hands on her hips.

"I've not seen you since summer."

"Oh, sorry." She hastily kissed both my cheeks before dragging Wren God knew where.

"It's nice to see the two of you together," said Z, approaching to stand next to me but with his back to the rest of the group. "We do need to chat."

"About?"

"An urgent matter." Z looked over his shoulder. I doubted he'd hesitate to speak in front of Shiver or Rivet. The duchess was an entirely different story.

"A moment?" I said to my brother.

Thankfully, our mother picked up on my tone and put her hand on Riv's arm. "I'll go join the girls, as they say."

Shiver led us into his study and closed the door. "You have the floor," he said to me.

"Z requested this chat," I said, motioning to Wren's father.

"While this would typically be out of reach for MI5, a situation involving a member of MI6 has been brought to my attention," Z said, clearing his throat.

"Out with it, Z. What's happened?" My impatience was reaching its limit.

"There's been a security breach."

I gripped the back of the chair in front of me. "How bad?"

"There's a chance Wren's Finley Harlow cover has been blown."

My grip on the chair tightened as the ramifications of Z's words raced through my mind.

"You believe this information was leaked from within MI6?"

"I'm certain of it. Thomason has been taken into custody."

"*Thomason*? When?"

Z pulled out his mobile. "Five minutes ago."

I looked between Z, Shiver, and Rivet. None of the three appeared surprised.

"A replacement needs to be named as quickly as possible, Wilder," said Rivet.

"Do you have a suggestion?"

"George."

I nodded. It was the name I'd expected.

"I'll take care of it," said Z.

"The breach itself needs to be addressed, Wild," said Shiver.

I nodded. "Before I bring this to Wren, I'd like to know how far-spread this is."

"There was also a breach in DHS," said Z.

"Sanborn?"

"Yes, and she's also in custody."

"Were they working together?"

"Yes," Z answered.

"Anyone else?"

"It appears United Russia may have had a hand in it. However, that has yet to be confirmed."

"Bloody hell."

"We'll know more once they've both been interrogated."

"While I'm not making light of the seriousness of the breach, isn't this something NGA should be handling?"

"In part. Vera is en route presently."

There was a knock at the door, and before any of us could respond, Wren burst in, mobile in hand.

"Excuse us, please," I said.

Shiver and Rivet left the room, but Z stayed.

"I should've killed her when I had the chance."

I raised a brow, trying to stifle a grin at her unexpected reaction. "When was that?"

"Every time I sat in her office and had to look at her smug face."

"This is serious, Wren," said Z.

"I know it is, but it's been a long time coming. Part of my decision as to whether I'd return to the NGA was what my role would be once my cover as Finley Harlow was blown. Now that it's happened, it'll be easier to make that determination."

Z rested his hand on her shoulder. I was close enough to reach out, but I waited, studying her responses, both verbal and nonverbal. The Wren I'd gotten a glimpse of in Cumbria was here in the room with us, and I couldn't wait to see what she'd do.

32

Wren

"Vera is on her way," I told Wilder and my father, who both nodded. "By here, I mean to the abbey."

There was a brief look of surprise on Wilder's face, but otherwise he appeared undaunted. "That was quick."

"She was already on her way to the UK," I explained. "My question is, how wise is it for us to meet with her here?"

"As in the abbey itself or on the estate?" he asked.

"Either."

"I see your concern. I'd be comfortable if you met at Dorchester House. If that's what you're asking."

"I am, but I want you to be a part of that meeting."

"Of course. After all, it is in part my fault that your identity has been compromised."

"It was inevitable." I looked at my father. "Thank you, Z. Would you mind please excusing us?"

"Certainly." He kissed the side of my face and left the study, closing the door behind him.

"How are you?" I asked Wilder.

"Me?" He laughed and pulled me into his arms. "My only concern is how you are."

"You said it's partially your fault this happened, but I disagree. I don't want you to feel as though you need to shoulder any blame. There isn't any blame, actually."

"What about Sanborn and Thomason?"

"I haven't been fully briefed on either yet—" I stopped mid-sentence.

"What's wrong?"

"I didn't sound like myself. At least the self I've been for the last few months. I told you earlier I'm not sure I can go back to that life."

"Whatever you want to do, I'll support," he said, cupping my face.

"What if that means I want to go back to Texas?"

"I'll learn to enjoy riding Western," he responded.

"Just like that."

Wilder took my hand and led me to the sofa. "I may be setting myself up for disappointment, but how were the last few months of your life?"

"It was nice to be in a place I thought of as home. Although, I have to admit to being bored. At least until Darrow arrived."

"I was given the promotion I thought I wanted more than anything. What I found out is, work isn't life."

"Are you saying you'd give up MI6?"

"If I had to choose between that and spending my life with you, then yes."

"Wilder, I don't know what to say."

"There's no hurry, Wren. Take however much time you need to make a decision about what you want to do."

"It makes me sound so selfish."

"I completely disagree. I'm the selfish one."

"What would MI6 do without you?"

"Z made a recommendation this morning that I wholeheartedly support. He suggested that Agent Marietta should step into Thomason's role. I intend to take that a step further and suggest she be named the next MI6 chief."

"Why?"

"Thomason was my second-in-command, and someone who I trusted in blind faith. Right there are grounds for my dismissal."

"You're being very hard on yourself, Wilder."

"I'm not so sure. I know that anyone not questioning my ability to lead, should probably be dismissed as well. In other words, Wren, my heart isn't in it."

"I'm back to not knowing what to say."

"I can make it easy for both of us by simply saying, I love you, Wren."

I smiled. "I love you, Wilder."

Those words didn't change my astonishment at both his willingness, seemingly with little thought, to leave MI6, as well as his self-recrimination in his role as chief.

There was a knock at the door; Wilder opened it.

"Am I interrupting?" asked Shiver.

"Yes," joked Wilder, motioning for him to come into the room.

"It's fine," I added. "You've heard Vera is on her way here as we speak."

"Our intention is for Wren to meet with her at Dorchester House."

"Good idea only in that we have a very full house presently."

"Was there something specific you wanted to discuss?" asked Wilder.

Shiver's brows raised as did mine. I hadn't seen much of the impatient side of Wilder except when he met me at the airport.

"I wanted to point out that Thomason worked for Rivet for over ten years, and more importantly, he was never once mentioned to replace him as chief."

Evidently, Shiver knew his brother would be carrying the blame for missing the agent's deceptions.

"Completely irrelevant, Shiv."

"What's to be done, then?" he asked, resting his hand on his brother's shoulder.

"Damage control," he answered, looking at me. "Ready to head to Dorchester House?"

Vera was at least two hours out, but I had no intention of saying so in front of Shiver. More than anything, I wanted time alone with Wilder in advance of the arrival of the woman I now considered my former boss.

"I'll ring later with an update."

Pinch was outside, standing by the car when Wilder and I came out.

"Been a long time since we've seen the Jag," he said, smirking.

"Sod off," responded Wilder. "Where's Darrow?"

Pinch ran his hand over his hair and shook his head. "Inside. We had another row." He looked up at me as though he perhaps wanted counsel, but when it came to Darrow, I had to stay out of it.

"Maybe we're forcing something that shouldn't be," he said, sounding more as though he was talking to himself than Wilder or me.

"I don't know, mate." Wilder shook his head.

"Heard there's a mess at MI6."

"Thomason."

"I know. I was part of the team investigating him."

Wilder's head shot up. "You didn't think to inform me?"

Pinch shook his head. "Couldn't. Orders."

"Let's go," said Wilder, ignoring Pinch's response. He opened my door and came right around to get in the driver's side of the car. Neither man said anything else.

Wilder didn't say a word on the way to Dorchester House either. Once he'd closed the front door behind us, he pulled me into his arms.

"Pinch was only doing his job."

I knew I had no business getting into the middle of the two men who had been friends most of their lives, but I felt compelled to defend Pinch. I'd been in the same position a number of times and resented being questioned about my loyalty when all I'd been doing is launching an investigation into someone who threatened to bring down part or all of my team.

"If truth be told, I'm embarrassed more than anything."

"Rivet is the one who should be embarrassed."

"I can't imagine you casting the same shade on Vera if this were happening inside of NGA."

"You're right."

"We're a pair, although I prefer the word team."

"I'll just freshen up before Vera gets here. If that's okay."

"Of course. I'll bring your bag up."

"I can get it, Wilder. There's next to nothing in it."

He put his hand on the back of my neck. "Allow me to be gallant, woman. My ego is sorely bruised at the moment."

He motioned for me to precede him when we got upstairs, but stopped me before I could turn into the room where I'd slept when I was here last. Instead, he led me down the hall.

His bedroom was what I'd expected based on the decor of the rest of the house. In contrast, it was the opposite style of his flat at Sky Gardens.

The head and footboard were made of dark-brown tufted leather. The bed itself was topped by an also dark comforter that was a Moroccan pattern of black and brown.

There was a gray chest at the foot of the bed and a divan made of the same color leather that sat in an angle near the fireplace. Two mahogany tables sat on either side of the bed, with gray lampshades that matched the divan and chest.

I would describe it as the quintessential bedroom for an English gentleman.

"As always, I'd love to know what your analytical mind is pondering."

I laughed. "Nothing really other than how much this room suits you."

When I came out of the bathroom, Wilder was lying on the bed with both hands behind his head.

"Come join me," he said, holding one hand out.

"I thought maybe you'd join me in the shower."

"I feel as though I haven't given you a moment's peace. Even now."

I snuggled into him and put my head above his heart. "I like it."

"When you hear what I'm about to propose, you may want to reflect on exactly how much time you think you can bear being around me."

I raised my head. "Wilder, I—"

"Hear me out, and know this, if I was about to propose something like marriage or even moving in together, you'd be right to turn me down flat based on lack of inspiration alone."

"What are you proposing?"

"What would you think about starting our own consulting business?"

I didn't answer right away, because I usually didn't. I preferred to give questions the consideration they were due based on their weight. In this case, it was heavy indeed. However, it was something I'd already considered—the consultant part at least. Partnering with Wilder hadn't been a consideration since I'd never dreamed he'd leave MI6.

"I like the idea."

"You do?" he asked, as though he was prepared for me to immediately reject the notion.

"Yes, and full disclosure, I'd considered a similar idea as means for me to be able to spend more time in London."

I smiled when he did. "You look entirely too pleased with yourself at the moment. Yes, Wilder, I did just admit to figuring out a way to stay here."

"What do you think of a partnership?"

"Again, to be honest, I think it's premature for you to be handing in your resignation."

"What if I can't imagine living that life anymore either?"

"I'll respect whatever you ultimately decide to do, in the same way you have already committed to supporting me. I've been away from the NGA for several months, which has given me a great deal more time to think about it." I startled at a loud noise coming from downstairs.

"That's the gate alert," he said. "Vera must have arrived."

I checked the time. "She's quite early."

"Let's see, shall we?"

Wilder got up and went downstairs, coming back up just as I finished dressing.

"She's pulling in now."

I raised a brow. "Did she fly here?"

Wilder laughed. "Actually, yes. She took a heli." Wilder pulled me into his arms. "Are you getting tired of me always having my hands on you?"

"Never."

He put both hands on my bottom and lifted me until my legs wrapped around his waist. "This is just to remind you what's coming after Vera leaves." He brought his lips to mine and kissed me hard.

I'd never get tired of kissing him either.

He angled his head, deepening our kiss, and then walked out of the bedroom, down the hallway, and to the stairs with me still in his arms.

I giggled. "Put me down."

He slid me down the length of his body, letting me feel exactly how much he wanted what would come after Vera's visit.

"What's she like, coffee or tea?" he asked, turning to go into the kitchen.

"Diet soda."

"Ugh, seriously?"

"She drinks it by the caseload."

"I have none."

I watched Vera's approach through the window. She'd aged in the months since I'd seen her, or maybe I just hadn't noticed it before.

When I opened the door, my mentor stepped forward to hug me. I wasn't certain how to react; it was something she'd never done before.

"Come in," I said, opening the door wider and taking a step back.

"Forgive my enthusiasm," said Vera. "You have no idea how much you've been missed."

I felt the air leave my lungs. This was not going to be an easy conversation, not that I'd expected it to be.

"What can I get you to drink? I'll warn you, Wilder doesn't keep diet soda in the house."

"Coffee, black, would be preferable anyway."

"I heard, and I'll be right out. Hello, Vera," Wilder shouted from the kitchen.

I led her into the sitting room where Wilder must've lit a fire when he came down earlier.

"This is lovely. It suits you."

"He suits me."

Vera leaned forward and took my hand. "I've known you a long time, and I've never seen you look so relaxed or so happy."

I felt my cheeks turn pink. "I am both."

"Which means, I suppose, you've made your decision."

"Is that why you've come? I thought it was to discuss the breach."

"It is, to a certain extent. I came prepared to offer you a deal to really get out if you wanted it."

"Meaning?"

"New identity. New life."

My eyes were wide, and I wished Wilder would hurry up and get in here with the coffee.

"Is that necessary?" I asked.

"Is what necessary?" asked Wilder. "Forgive me. Nosy beau. If it isn't any of my business, please say so." He leaned over and kissed Vera's cheek before handing her the coffee.

I looked between them. "You two know each other?"

"Not for long," Vera answered. "Only since last February."

I continued looking from one to the other.

"I demanded an audience," explained Wilder.

I turned to Vera. "You never said."

"I called you in to tell you, and before I could, you issued the edict that if I wanted you to stay in NGA's employ, there were certain guidelines that needed to be followed 'to the letter.'"

"Ugh, I did say those precise words, didn't I?"

"She did," Vera said to Wilder. "Emphasis on 'to the letter.'"

"She can be a demanding little thing." He winked and sat on the arm of my chair. "When I came in, you were asking Vera if something was necessary."

"Right. She came to offer me a new identity."

"As in witness protection?" he asked.

"In a way. Mainly, if Kennedy King wanted to disappear, I could make it happen."

"I'll reiterate Wren's earlier question. Is that necessary?"

"It's one option among many. Which leads me to ask, have you made a decision?"

I looked up at Wilder. "I believe we have."

"Out with it," he said, smiling and nudging me.

I rested my arm on his leg. "Wilder and I have been discussing forming a consultancy."

"You're serious?"

"We are," he answered for us both. "In light of the breach, I've decided not to accept the position of permanent chief, not that I anticipate it will be offered."

"That's more than a little rash, don't you think? What is it with you Whittakers? As soon as that desk job gets a little too close, you resign."

"I can't speak for my brother; however, I got a glimpse of the life, and it didn't appeal."

"Very well," said Vera, standing.

"You don't have to leave so quickly," I said, stunned by Vera's abruptness.

"I'm not leaving. I've been invited to the abbey once our meeting concluded. Don't you all speak to one another?"

"Before you go, can I ask? What about Sanborn?"

"She's in custody, not that she was ever out of it. We let her go to see if she'd lead us to the people we were really after."

"And who was that?" Wilder asked.

"Thomason, obviously. From what we've been able to piece together, the two made contact when

Wren's trip was in the planning stages. We still don't know if they already knew one another or if they were put together by a third party." She looked from me to Wilder.

"Who else did she lead you to?" I asked.

Vera smiled. "You've had time to think about it. Any theories?"

"A couple."

Vera rubbed her hands together and sat back down. "I can't wait to hear." She winked at Wilder when I stood and paced in front of the fireplace.

"The first is Kruchenko."

"Why?" Vera asked.

"He had known ties to Mormeht Savat." The man whose execution I'd arranged in January.

Vera nodded. "Why else?"

"He's Ukrainian, and we all know that after the United States, they are Russia's greatest enemy. He's deep enough into intelligence that he could easily have masterminded the entire thing with the PKK in an effort to undermine Russia's deal with Turkey."

"I'm with you so far."

I looked at Wilder. "Do you know what kind of access Thomason would've had to Matthew?"

"Unlimited."

"Prior to him being imprisoned?"

"Again, unlimited. For all intents and purposes, Matthew was Rivet's son. I'm sure he came and went at MI6 with some regularity."

"Was Thomason aware of Matthew's true parentage?" I asked.

Wilder nodded. "I'd say it's likely."

"I believe Thomason's initial involvement with Matthew was unrelated to the Russian-Turkish deal," I told them. "It had to have been going on for months if not years."

"Anyone fancy something stronger than coffee?" Wilder asked, standing and running his hand through his hair.

"Sure," I answered absentmindedly.

"Vera?"

"What the hell."

33

Wilder

I pulled out Wellie's brandy, poured a heavy shot, downed it, and then poured another along with one for Wren and Vera.

Watching Wren process what I guessed Vera already knew, was as fascinating as it was daunting. In my role at MI6, I had access to the highest level of intelligence, but I didn't keep it in my head like Wren did.

She'd said she hadn't "kept up" in the last several months, yet she remembered details that never would've been on my radar.

Could she really give up her life at the NGA? Wren seemed to come alive, blossoming, once Vera asked if she had any theories. She'd give it all up to be with me, I knew that, but could I allow her to?

"How did it come together?" I heard Vera ask Wren when I came back in the room with our drinks.

"Thank you," Wren said, leaning forward to kiss me when I handed her the glass. "Are you okay? I know it's difficult to talk about Matthew and everything that happened."

"I'm fine. Truly." My eyes met Vera's, and I wondered if she knew my discomfort was based more on Wren's extraordinary abilities rather than the fact that my half brother had tried to kill my siblings and me.

"Wren was just telling me her theory of what happened between Thomason and Caird."

"Matthew, she means," Wren said unnecessarily.

I stood near her with my elbow on the fireplace mantel. "Don't stop on my account. I'm anxious to hear your thoughts."

"Rivet made no secret that he was ready to retire. My thinking is that Thomason was disappointed when he was passed over in favor of Merrigan Shaw, but Rivet offering her the position was something everyone in the intelligence world expected."

"I agree," I said, smiling at the beautiful and brilliant woman standing before me.

Wren continued. "When Merrigan turned the job down and Rivet tapped Shiver, Thomason was no longer disappointed; he was angry. Depending on how long he'd known about Matthew's true parentage, maybe he'd already begun to fuel that flame."

"You're saying he convinced my already unstable and mentally ill half brother to take matters into his own hands and eliminate my father's other heirs?"

"This is all conjecture for now, but I can see it as one scenario."

"I can as well."

"The two of you make a good team," said Vera, who I'd almost forgotten was in the room. "Kruchenko, in his position with Ukrainian intelligence, would have known about Matthew's rampage at Whittaker Abbey and what his intended outcome was."

"Right," said Wren. "Kruchenko would also have come in contact with Nate Thomason as part of both of their positions." She put her hand on mine. "Sanborn made no secret of her issues with you. It would be easy to imagine that she and Thomason discussed you if they did, in fact, make the arrangements for my visit."

"It may be years before we know all of the intricacies of what actually led to today's outcome," commented Vera. "Suffice to say that between them all, the only thing they actually managed to achieve was Matthew Caird's death. If your theory is right, Wren, and I believe it is, whatever their combined agendas were, along with their personal ones, they failed miserably."

She took a long drink of Wellie's brandy and then coughed a little.

"Sorry, I should've warned you. It's a bit potent."

"I'm made of pretty tough stuff, Whittaker," said Vera, setting her empty glass on the table. She folded her hands on her lap and looked at Wren. "Please continue."

With the rapt attention of both Vera and me, Wren continued to outline most of what we already knew.

The deal between Russia and Turkey for the former's air defense system, which Kruchenko tried to put a stop to, had gone through.

Mormeht Savat's death severely crippled the PKK, and Turkey, no longer defenseless against their air attacks, brought the rest of the organization down, and thus, eliminated a terrorist cell that had been a strong ally of Ukraine.

While United Russia remained a threat to the US as well as much of the rest of the world, their historical roller-coaster ride of power began and ended with a specific leader. Once the current president was either dead or overthrown by yet another revolution, it was impossible to say whether they would remain a world power.

"And that, my friend, is how it's done," said Vera, standing to put her hand on Wren's arm. "It's fascinating to watch, isn't it?" she said to me.

"She says her brilliance isn't close to your level."

Vera laughed. "Oh, Wren. If you only knew your own worth. On that subject, whenever you have your consultancy established, NGA would like to put you on retainer."

"Where is Kruchenko?" I asked Vera, walking her to the door.

"Already in the US so we won't have a repeat of Matthew's pesky extradition fight."

"That fight brought Wren to me."

"You can thank me for that."

I took Vera's hand and kissed the back of it. "I can never thank you enough."

"Take good care of her, or you'll answer to me."

I smiled. "I'll guard her like the goddess she is."

"See to it. Will you and Wren be at dinner?"

"Yes. We'll join you at the abbey shortly," I said, waving her off.

"How are you doing?" I asked, joining Wren in the sitting room.

"Exhausted."

"If we became consultants, it would be more of the same."

"That's what I was thinking. I told you before I'm not sure I can go back to that life. But, Wilder, even if we don't start our own firm, I can still stay in England."

"I can leave England as well." I pulled her into my arms. "As I've said at least twice before, this is nothing that needs to be decided now."

34

Wren

Over dinner, I watched Darrow with Pinch. It wasn't the first time I'd seen them together, but they didn't seem as happy as they had the night I'd joined them, Shiver and Orina, and Wilder for dinner at the pub.

I really hoped it wasn't because of Quint. I couldn't see my brother ever settling down. Not that I knew if that was what Darrow would want anyway.

It didn't help that Vera was seated between Pinch and Z and the three were conversing about the recent MI6 and DHS turmoil while speaking in the cryptic language those in intelligence often used.

"Darrow?" I said. "Would you like to take a walk between courses?"

"Yes. I'd love it," she answered, scooting her chair away from the table before Pinch could get up and do it for her.

We'd just gotten out the door when I saw Vera following us.

"I owe you an apology," she said to Darrow. "I was monopolizing the conversation."

"It's all right," Darrow said, not looking at the woman who'd apologized.

"It isn't. It was rude."

When Darrow didn't respond, I made eye contact with Vera, who nodded when I motioned toward the house with my head.

"What's wrong?" I asked once Darrow and I were alone.

"It isn't the same as it used to be between Pinch and me."

"Could it be better?"

"It could, but it isn't."

"Darrow, I hope my brother doesn't play into this in any way. Quint isn't exactly…"

"What? Finish what you were going to say about him."

"He isn't the relationship type."

Darrow raised a brow. "I've never met someone who treats a woman the way your brother does."

I was afraid to ask what she meant. When we were in high school, Quint was definitely the love-them-and-leave-them type.

"He's a gentleman. Your brother would never leave me sitting there while he spent the entire dinner talking to the woman seated on the other side of him."

"I don't know what to say about that."

"The thing between Axel and me has run its course."

"You don't know; it might still work out."

Darrow stopped walking. "Are you opposed to my relationship with your brother?"

I stopped too. "I'm not. However, I was there when we got off the plane, and you were very happy to see Axel. I have to admit I was glad Quint wasn't there to see it."

"We've known each other since we were children. Sometimes it's more like he's my brother."

"And sometimes it's not."

She shrugged. "I was the only person at the table who had no clue what everyone else was talking about. Even my mother understood what was going on."

"It's difficult when everyone else is talking shop. I'll be mindful we don't do so much of that when we go back in."

"I've a headache anyway. Maybe I'll stop in and see Wellie before I go back to Covington House."

"I wish you would come back inside with me instead."

"Remember when I told you I never wanted to come back to England?"

I nodded.

"I had my reasons."

I watched Darrow walk away, unsure if I should let her go or continue trying to get her to come back for the rest of dinner.

"Where's she off to?" asked Wilder, coming up behind me.

"She was bored, so she's going to see Wellie."

"It's always been my sister's lot. Most times she has no idea what any of us are talking about, and that's by design."

"I'm worried about her."

Wilder spun me around so I was facing him, and kissed me.

"What was that for?"

"Because you care about Darrow, and I love that about you."

"I didn't help. She still left."

"But she left knowing someone noticed."

"Why didn't Pinch notice? That's what she really wanted."

"I don't know," he said, drawing me to him. "Maybe it's run its course."

"That's what she said."

When we went back inside, it was as though Pinch hadn't even noticed Darrow was gone. If that's the way he was with her all the time, then maybe it was time for her to move on. My only worry was, would Quint be any different?

"What's your plan?" asked Shiver once we'd said good night to Vera and Z, who were sharing a ride back to London with Rivet and Victoria.

"That is a question with a wide range of answers," I responded.

"Will you go back to NGA?"

"I don't think so."

"What are you grilling my woman about?" asked Wilder, coming back from thanking Mrs. Mollybock for making dinner for the crowd.

"That's why she likes him so much, you know," said Shiver. "He's the only one who ever remembers to thank her for doing her job."

"You would've made a terrible chief," said Wilder.

"You're right. I would've. What of you? Still thinking of turning it down?"

Wilder looked at me before answering. "We have a lot to figure out yet," he said. "However, right now, we're going back to Dorchester House."

"Do you plan to stay for very long?"

"I know what he's getting at," Wilder whispered. "He wants to know if he can con me into going out and getting the trees since Wellie is under the weather."

"You saw right through me."

"Trees?" I asked.

"The duchess has always insisted on each of the 'public rooms,' as she calls them, having a decorated tree."

"How many is that?"

"One year it was twenty."

"Cor blimey," I muttered.

Shiver laughed and so did Wilder. "You're one of us now, my darling."

35

Wilder
Christmas

"Thank goodness Losha put her foot down with Mother over Christmas trees this year," said Darrow, sitting with Wren and me over morning tea and coffee at the abbey.

"How did she manage it?" I asked.

"She said it would be too confusing for Kazmir."

"And that worked?" asked Wren.

"He's her first grandchild. She'd do anything for him and Lilliya."

"Where's Pinch this morning?"

"I've no idea," my sister answered.

"That's off again, then?"

She nodded, taking another sip of coffee. "Been off for quite a while, brother."

"I can't keep up."

I sneaked a peek at Wren, who was looking at the ornaments on the tree, seemingly not paying attention to the conversation.

I slung my arm around her shoulders. "What are you waiting for, darling? Did you have a question for Darrow?"

"I'm not sure it's the right time."

"For what?" Darrow asked.

Wren held out the hand she'd been strategically hiding from my sister since she came in the room. "I was wondering if you'd be my maid of honor."

As I'd expected, Darrow's shrieks of joy had everyone running to see what the fuss was about. Between the crowd of people hugging her and shaking my hand, my beautiful bride-to-be and I were on separate sides of the room, but our eyes stayed fixated on one another.

"I love you," I said over the din of my family and her father, whose permission I'd asked the night before last.

"A Christmas Eve engagement! How romantic," said the duchess, who looked over at Rivet.

I had a feeling they had their own announcement to make, but wouldn't steal the spotlight from Wren. I walked over and put my arm around my mother and kissed her cheek. "Thank you, Duchess."

"Whatever for?" she asked, winking.

"I don't want to keep you from celebrating your own happiness."

"Today is your day, Sutton," she whispered.

Rivet stood behind me and clapped my back. "I understand your resignation from SIS is official?"

"That's right."

"Congratulations," he said, shaking my hand.

"Not exactly the reaction I expected."

"There's an announcement to be made soon, I understand."

"George?"

Rivet shook his head and motioned to the other side of the room where Wren stood, talking to her father.

"Z?"

"That's right."

"I had no idea. He didn't mention it."

"He and Pinch are credited with taking down Thomason. What's more, between Z and Vera, Wren's true identity and the role she played in the intelligence world was well contained."

"Who's taking over MI5?"

"It's a tossup between Pinch and George."

"Bugger me. That's not good. They're vying?"

"May the best man win, so to speak."

"Where is Pinch anyway?" I asked.

"I was going to ask the same of you," answered Rivet.

"Perhaps he's at Wellie's."

"Darrow?" Shiver called out to her from the entryway.

"Yes?"

"You have a caller."

"What's this, then?" muttered Rivet when she left the room.

"No idea."

Moments later, we heard her squeal of delight. "Quint? I can't believe you're here!"

Wren came over to me. "I can assure you, I knew nothing about this."

"Good bloody thing her and Pinch are on the outs," I whispered.

"I hear congratulations are in order," Wren's brother said after walking in, hugging Wren, and shaking my hand. "I'm Quint Alexander."

"Wilder Whittaker."

"What are you doing here, and how did you know about our engagement?" Wren asked, looking over at Z.

"Yes, Z filled me in, but to be honest, I was worried about you."

"Why?"

"We haven't spoken since right after Thanksgiving."

"It isn't like we do that kind of thing, Quint."

He laughed and motioned toward Darrow. "She's acting surprised, but I was invited."

"That's my sister," I said, rolling my eyes. Later I'd have a talk with the little imp. As I'd said to Wren a few minutes earlier, it was a damn good thing she and Pinch were on the outs.

"When's the wedding?" Quint asked.

"We're keeping it very small. Pretty much limited to everyone in the room," Wren answered.

"Okay, when?"

"Um…New Year's Eve."

I caught the flash of hurt in Quint's eyes, which he quickly masked. It was interesting how younger siblings often doubted whether the older had much interest in them. Wren had assumed that her older brother wouldn't care about being at her wedding. It was something Wren and I had in common. There were many times I'd assumed Shiver couldn't care less about my life when in actuality, he cared very much.

"Will you be able to stay for it?" she asked.

"Couldn't get me to leave."

There was another commotion coming from the entryway. "Who else are we expecting?" I murmured to no one in particular.

"Wellie! What a wonderful surprise," I heard Shiver say in a voice that was louder than necessary. "And, Axel, we had no idea you'd be joining us. Come in, come in."

"Oh, my," whispered Wren, giggling.

Darrow turned around and pushed her.

"Don't start. If you start, I'll start."

"These two," said Quint. "They get the giggles at the most inappropriate times."

Wren and I stood back, watching Darrow, Quint, and Pinch as they attempted civility in the midst of terrific awkwardness.

"Quint knows about Pinch. I don't know if it's the same the other way around."

"He should be able to figure it out, given his profession, my darling."

"I'm glad he can stay for the wedding."

"You're sure you want to do it this quickly?"

Wren turned her back to the room and put her arms around my waist. "I'd marry you right now if there was a magistrate here."

"What's your rush?" I asked, leaning down to kiss beneath her ear.

"The sooner we're married, the sooner we can leave for the Maldives."

"Two weeks on Meeru Island. I fear you'll grow bored."

"That's your challenge, isn't it? To see to it I don't."

"Challenge accepted, my precious little bird."

Epilogue

Wren

New Year's Eve

"How are you doing?" asked Darrow, fussing with my hair.

I laughed. "You're more nervous than I am."

"You're right. I am."

I set my bouquet of flowers on the bed and took Darrow's hands in mine. "You haven't been yourself since Christmas. Before that actually. Not since the dinner you left in the middle of."

"I don't know what you're talking about."

"You invited my brother to England for Christmas without even mentioning it to me."

"I didn't want you to talk me out of it."

"That's an honest response. Are you feeling okay?"

"I'm fine, just ready for the holidays to be over."

"Then what happens?"

"Meaning?"

"When is Quint leaving?"

Darrow bit her lip. "I'm not certain."

"I see."

I watched my friend's expression change. "Can we please focus? You are about to marry my brother."

"Yes, I am about to marry him." I smiled, picked up my bouquet, and closed my eyes. By the time the clock struck midnight, I would be Mrs. Sutton Whittaker. I never dreamed we'd find our way back to each other, but we had. "I love him so much," I murmured.

"I'd give anything to feel the way you do now," Darrow whispered.

"You will," I said, squeezing her hand. "When the time is right."

"I doubt it will ever be."

"As did I, and look at us."

"Just make sure I catch the bouquet."

"You're the only single woman at the wedding. I'll just hand it to you."

"My mother."

"Right. Well, she isn't really single. Plus, she's already been married, so she's ineligible."

"Thanks, Wren," said Darrow with tears in her eyes.

"Why are you crying?"

"You're the best friend I've ever had. I'm going to miss you so much."

"Don't make me cry. I assure you, it won't be pretty." I dabbed at the corners of my eyes with my handkerchief. "And we aren't going to be away that long. A month is all."

Darrow nodded, but there was something she wasn't telling me; however, five minutes before I was supposed to descend the grand staircase in Whittaker Abbey to marry the love of my life wasn't the time to get into it.

"Ready?"

"It was a beautiful wedding," said Wilder's mother as we were saying good night.

"Thank you, ma'am," I responded.

"Please call me Victoria."

"Yes, ma'am," I said and then laughed. "I mean Victoria."

"You're leaving tomorrow, then?"

Wilder put his arm around my shoulders. "Just after brunch in town. You're under no obligation to attend if you have other plans."

"My son got married this evening. What other plans would I have?"

"Perhaps a wedding of your own?"

"Pish posh," she answered, swatting at him. "We'll elope and save you all the embarrassment."

"It's nice to see you so happy, Duchess."

"And the two of you."

After carrying me over the threshold of Dorchester House, Wilder lit a fire and brought in two glasses of Wellie's brandy.

"We survived an entire week without a serious brawl between your brother and Pinch. I'm amazed," he said, handing me a glass.

"What was your sister thinking?"

"I cannot tell you how many times I've asked myself the same question. Do you think your brother realized what was going on?"

"He isn't blind, Wilder."

"Yes, well, there was the murderous glare Pinch fixed on him whenever they were in the same room."

"I'm just glad he's leaving tomorrow morning."

"Same time we are, or close, right?"

"I don't know. He just said tomorrow when I asked. And honestly, right at this moment, there is only one thing I care about."

"And that is?"

"Mr. Whittaker, unless you are prepared to close all the draperies in this room, I highly suggest you take me upstairs immediately."

Wilder finished the brandy in his glass. "Just because we're married, does not change who makes the rules, my beautiful bride," he said, lifting me into his arms.

"What in the world?" said Wilder when both of our phones' as well as the house phone's ringing woke us up the next morning. "They couldn't just have brunch without us?"

At the same time, we heard someone pounding on the door.

"You get the phone; I'll get the door," said Wilder, pulling on a pair of pants.

"Hello? Z? What's going on?" I said, answering my father's call.

"Did you happen to speak with Darrow last night before you and Wilder left the abbey?"

"Not other than to say good night and we'd see her in the morning."

"Brunch. Right. Thanks, sweetheart."

"Z? What's going on?"

"Nothing, I'm sure. She's probably already in town."

I could hear him saying the same thing to someone in the background.

"I'll call you back," he said, ending the call.

I put on a robe and went downstairs. "Z just called, looking for Darrow," I said, coming around the corner to find both Quint and Pinch in the sitting room. "What's wrong?"

Wilder, running a hand through his hair, turned around and put his arm around me.

"Darrow's gone missing."

"What? No, I was just talking with Z, and he said she probably went into town early." I looked between Quint and Pinch. "Who saw her last?"

"We both did," answered Quint.

"Well? Where were you?"

"It was shortly after the two of you left. I went looking for her…" said Quint.

"And found her with me," added Pinch.

"What happened then?" asked Wilder.

Neither Quint nor Pinch responded.

"What bloody happened?" yelled Wilder.

"We got into a bit of a pissing match," said Pinch.

"Darrow tried to break it up, but neither of us was paying much attention to her."

"Her last words before she stormed out were 'I never want to see either of you again.'"

"You didn't go after her?" I asked my brother, who shook his head.

"Or you?" Wilder asked Pinch.

"We actually proceeded to get quite wankered."

"What do you mean you got wankered?" asked Wilder, yelling again.

"You know how she is, Wild," said Pinch.

"Where do you think she would've gone?" Quint asked.

"Have you checked Wellie's?" asked Wilder.

"Not there. He reported not having seen her once he left your wedding party."

"And you checked the abbey. She didn't just go sleep it off in a room there?"

"If she's there, we haven't been able to find her."

I took Wilder's hand and pulled him out of the room. "Has she done anything like this before?"

Wilder nodded. "She left without telling a soul she was going to see you."

"She had to have told someone. Z delivered her."

"Yes, he was her ally in that foray."

"He doesn't know where she is now, though. I just got off the phone with him."

"Bloody hell," muttered Wilder.

"What about friends? Cousins? Other family?"

"It's an endless list of possibilities," he answered. "Let's just hope she's located before our flight."

I stared into my husband's eyes.

"I know that look. What are you thinking, darling?"

"I'm sorry, Wilder, but we can't leave until we find your sister."

Keep reading for a preview

of the next book in the

Royal Agents of MI6 series—

Feel My Pinch!

1

Pinch

"Bugger me," I seethed when I heard the pub door open and saw the woman coming in.

"Who's that?" asked my best mate, Wilder. He and I had grown up together on his family's estate. Now, we worked together for SIS, Her Majesty's Secret Service—I was with MI5 and he had recently resigned from MI6.

"Bloody reporter," I answered, running my hand over my shortly cropped hair.

"Looks familiar."

"Ms. Cartwright works for the *Times.* She's also friends with your sister."

"She's on her way over here," Wilder warned.

"If there's anyone I'd like to walk into this pub less than the devil himself, it's her."

"Why?"

"She almost brought down my last investigation. Not to mention, she's been snooping around about Wren."

"Bugger me," muttered Wilder, repeating my earlier words and leaving me to join his wife and her brother at their table.

Wren was a former secret agent for the United States National Security Agency, whose identity had been compromised by a leak at the UK's Secret Intelligence Service—otherwise known as MI6. To make matters worse, the security breach had happened while Wilder was serving as the international section's interim chief.

Through the combined efforts of MI6 and MI5, the UK's domestic counter-intelligence and security agency, we'd been able to mitigate the threat caused by her exposure. However, the last thing we needed now was someone like Ms. Cartwright poking her nose in it.

Wren and Wilder had both resigned from their respective jobs right after they got married, in order to start a private intelligence consultancy. First, though, they were honeymooning in the Maldives for two weeks. The gathering tonight was to wish the couple a *bon voyage.*

When I heard someone clear her throat, I turned around to find Ms. Cartwright standing directly in front of me.

"Is that Wren Whittaker, or should I say Kennedy King?" she asked, looking beyond me to the table where Wilder and Wren were seated.

I leaned down and got right in her face. "Who she is or isn't, is none of your bloody business. You report one word about anyone in the Whittaker family, and I'll see to it that you're imprisoned for treason—that's if I can't manage to kill you first."

I backed away, folded my arms, and waited for her response.

"Okay, okay. You don't have to be so threaten-y. You know I found out through Darrow."

Darrow. Wilder's younger sister and my former "girlfriend." Although with as many times as we'd been on and off and then on again in the last few months, it was hard to keep track of which we were at any given time.

"Have you found her?" Ms. Cartwright asked, bringing up yet another subject I had no intention of discussing with her.

"No comment."

"Off the record, then. You know she and I have been mates since primary school."

The concern I saw in the woman's eyes was genuine enough that I shook my head.

"She's been gone a week's time now, right?"

To be precise, it had been ten days since Darrow Whittaker disappeared from her residence on the estate that had been in her family for generations, five days since I found her, and three days since she disappeared again, only this time with my help.

Of course I couldn't talk about any of it with someone outside of her family, especially not a reporter.

"I know how upsetting this must be for you."

I looked down where her hand rested on my forearm, growling as I wrenched it away. Having concern was one thing; gumshoeing was another.

"The ice you're walking on is exceedingly thin. I suggest you turn around and leave of your own volition, unless you'd prefer I toss you over my shoulder and carry you out."

"Wait, I have another—"

I leaned my shoulder into Ms. Cartwright's stomach and wrapped my arm around the back of her knees. As threatened, I tossed her over my shoulder and carried her out to the pavement.

"What are you doing?" she screeched, pounding on my back. When she tried to kick her legs, I tightened my hold.

I made eye contact with one of several agents also at the pub to bid farewell to Wilder and Wren, who nodded in acknowledgment as I unceremoniously set her feet-first on the pavement in front of the pub.

"Go home!" I spat, turning to go back in. I heard her shout at me to wait, but I ignored her.

Once back inside, I needed a minute before joining the party. I pulled out a stool at the bar, ordered a pint, and took a deep breath. Not the smartest thing I could've done, given the beguiling reporter's scent lingered on my skin.

"I'll take a whiskey," I said to the barmaid.

"Looks like you need a double," she responded, setting a glass and the bottle in front of me.

With such close proximity to Vauxhall Cross, otherwise known as SIS headquarters, the pub's staff were trained not to ask questions of their patrons. They did, however, seem to innately know when one of their regulars needed an extra shot or, in this case, two or three.

It wasn't this specific run-in with Ms. Cartwright that had me rattled. I could handle the reporter side of her. It was the female beneath the ink slinger's tough exterior that got under my skin.

I tried my damnedest not to look at her pouty, bee-stung lips or let myself think about how much I wanted to lick off the bright-red lipstick she wore.

I raised the glass, inhaling her scent again as I tossed the drink back. The woman smelled like none other I'd ever known—as mysterious and provocative as spicy and floral.

Today her long sandy-blonde hair was pulled back from her face in a tight bun. She wore a dark-colored pencil skirt that skimmed her knees, a loose-fitting white silk blouse that did nothing other than accentuate her mouthwatering curves, and the sexiest damn black heels I'd ever seen.

Having her in my arms, albeit slung over my shoulder, almost did me in. I longed to take her home, strip her bare, and linger over every scrumptious inch of the body that so regularly invaded my dreams.

"Bugger me," I muttered as I had when she walked through the door earlier. Esland Cartwright wasn't just an annoying reporter on my beat, she was one of Darrow's best mates, and that meant hands off.

About the Author

USA Today and Amazon Top 15 Bestselling Author Heather Slade writes shamelessly sexy, edge-of-your seat romantic suspense.

She gave herself the gift of writing a book for her own birthday one year. Forty-plus books later (and counting), she's having the time of her life.

The women Slade writes are self-confident, strong, with wills of their own, and hearts as big as the Colorado sky. The men are sublimely sexy, seductive alphas who rise to the challenge of capturing the sweet soul of a woman whose heart they'll hold in the palm of their hand forever. Add in a couple of neck-snapping twists and turns, a page-turning mystery, and a swoon-worthy HEA, and you'll be holding one of her books in your hands.

She loves to hear from my readers. You can contact her at heather@heatherslade.com

To keep up with her latest news and releases, please visit her website at www.heatherslade.com to sign up for her newsletter.

MORE FROM AUTHOR HEATHER SLADE

BUTLER RANCH
Kade's Worth
Brodie's Promise
Maddox's Truce
Naughton's Secret
Mercer's Vow
Kade's Return
Butler Ranch Christmas

WICKED WINEMAKERS FIRST LABEL
Brix's Bid
Ridge's Release
Press' Passion
Zin's Sins
Tryst's Temptation

WICKED WINEMAKERS SECOND LABEL
Beau's Beloved
Coming Soon:
Cru's Crush
Bones' Bliss
Snapper's Seduction
Kick's Kiss

ROARING FORK RANCH
Coming Soon:
Roaring Fork Wrangler
Roaring Fork Roughstock
Roaring Fork Rockstar
Roaring Fork Rooker
Roaring Fork Bridger

THE ROYAL AGENTS OF MI6
Make Me Shiver
Drive Me Wilder
Feel My Pinch
Chase My Shadow
Find My Angel

K19 SECURITY SOLUTIONS TEAM ONE
Razor's Edge
Gunner's Redemption
Mistletoe's Magic
Mantis' Desire
Dutch's Salvation

K19 SECURITY SOLUTIONS TEAM TWO
Striker's Choice
Monk's Fire
Halo's Oath
Tackle's Honor
Onyx's Awakening

K19 SHADOW OPERATIONS TEAM ONE
Code Name: Ranger
Code Name: Diesel
Code Name: Wasp
Code Name: Cowboy
Code Name: Mayhem

K19 ALLIED INTELLIGENCE TEAM ONE
Code Name: Ares
Code Name: Cayman
Code Name: Poseidon
Code Name: Zeppelin
Code Name: Magnet

K19 ALLIED INTELLIGENCE TEAM TWO
Coming Soon:
Code Name: Puck
Code Name: Michelangelo
Code Name: Typhon
Code Name: Hornet
Code Name: Reaper

PROTECTORS UNDERCOVER
Undercover Agent
Undercover Emissary
Coming Soon:
Undercover Savior
Undercover Infidel
Undercover Assassin

THE INVINCIBLES TEAM ONE
Decked
Edged
Grinded
Riled
Smoked

THE INVINCIBLES TEAM TWO
Bucked
Irished
Sainted
Hammered
Ripped

THE UNSTOPPABLES TEAM ONE
Furied
Merried

COWBOYS OF CRESTED BUTTE
A Cowboy Falls
A Cowboy's Dance
A Cowboy's Kiss
A Cowboy Stays
A Cowboy Wins

www.ingramcontent.com/pod-product-compliance
Lightning Source LLC
Chambersburg PA
CBHW070617300726
48975CB00006B/1847